FENELLA J. MILLER

DUKE IN DANGER

Complete and Unabridged

LINFORD
Leicester

First published in Great Britain in 2019

First Linford Edition
published 2020

A catalogue record for this book is available
from the British Library.

ISBN 978–1–4448–4397–2

Published by
F. A. Thorpe (Publishing)
Anstey, Leicestershire

Set by Words & Graphics Ltd.
Anstey, Leicestershire
Printed and bound in Great Britain by
T. J. International Ltd., Padstow, Cornwall

This book is printed on acid-free paper

DUKE IN DANGER

Lady Helena Faulkner agrees to marry only if her indulgent parents can find a gentleman who fits her exacting requirements. Wild and unconventional, she has no desire for romance, but wants a friend who will let her live as she pleases. Lord Christopher Drake, known to Helena as Kit, her brother's best friend, needs a rich wife to support his mother and siblings. It could be the perfect arrangement. But when malign forces do their best to separate them, can Helena and Kit overcome the disasters and find true happiness?

Prologue

Andover Hall, April 1810

The Duke of Andover had not long to live. He had summoned his lawyers to his bedside and they were now fully cognisant of his status. His doctor sat anxiously at his bedside, warning him that any exertion would shorten what little time he had left. There was something the dying man had to resolve before he went to meet his maker. Richard, known as The Marquis of Barkham, did not look overly pleased to be standing at his father's deathbed.

The duke smiled to himself. His son would be even less pleased when he knew why he was there. The quacks had given the duke a week at the most before his heart gave up. The old man prayed that would be long enough to put something right that he should

1

never have agreed to, all those years ago.

He raised his hand and immediately had the full attention of those surrounding him. He was used to having his slightest wish obeyed. His son had known from the moment he was born that he was destined to be the Duke of Andover. He had been spoiled by his mother until her death, given everything he wanted and denied nothing. This had not, with hindsight, been a sensible course of action. The young man staring disdainfully down at him was not a son one could be proud of.

If Richard had been the kind of young man who would inherit his wealth and status with humility, would honour the family name, then none of this would have been necessary. However, the duke was not so blind to his own son's faults that he did not know where his duty lay. The gentleman, if he could be designated as such, who stood no more than two yards from him, was a rakehell, a debaucher of young women, an inveterate gambler who would bring ruin and destruction to the family if he ever got his hands on the inheritance.

'Richard, I have something to tell you. I am a twin. I had an identical brother, Richard, who was born five minutes before me. He was everything to me, so when he fell in love with a young lady deemed unsuitable to be a duchess, he begged me to change places with him.'

His son's expression was murderous. This was going better than he'd expected.

'I am not the Duke of Andover. I am Simon, Lord Drake. The title is not yours, any more than it is mine. My brother died many years ago and I lost touch with his widow and her family. He left a son and it is he who will inherit the dukedom and all it entails. My lawyers are now scouring the countryside for my nephew to give him the good news.'

He had expected Richard to rant and roar on receiving this unexpected and exceedingly unpleasant information. What he had not anticipated was that his son would laugh.

'Good God, sir, I have never heard such nonsense. The ramblings of a dying man. Do you honestly think my grandfather would not have known of such a deception as you describe?'

Their mother had died in a carriage accident when they were in leading strings and there was no one employed at Andover Hall who had been there longer than a decade. He and Richard had made very sure that the deception would remain undetected and permanent. He was breaking his solemn vow by revealing it now.

He closed his eyes and breathed as steadily as he could through his nose, trying to slow the frantic beating of his failing heart. He should never have left things to the last minute. He had known for years that Richard should never be allowed to inherit the title.

As the light faded he heard his son laughing. This was the last sound he heard before he drew his final breath.

1

Faulkner Court, Essex.
May 1810

'Lady Helena Faulkner, I shall not tell you a second time. Your papa has been waiting to speak to you this past hour whilst you have been out here climbing trees.'

'Mama, I am coming directly. Is he very cross?'

Her mother smiled indulgently. 'No, my love, not very. However, he has an ultimatum for you and you would do well to agree.'

Helena dropped the last six feet to the ground and hugged her parent. 'I am a sore trial to you both, I am well aware of that. I know that you both have my best interests at heart, wish to see me settled before I am at my last prayers . . . '

'Good heavens, my dear, hardly that. Admittedly two and twenty is somewhat older than one would like one's daughter to be before she is married, but you are so very beautiful and impossibly rich, that I doubt your maturity will be a handicap.'

'I have no intention of parading around a ballroom for the inspection of any gentlemen so you can forget about suggesting I attend the next Season.'

They had now entered the palatial building that was the Faulkner ancestral home and the only place in the world she wished to be. Why should she give up her independence, her freedom, to be at the beck and call of a gentleman she did not know? Not to mention the fact that she might find herself producing an infant every year. She was not overfond of children.

The earl, her dearest papa, was not striding about his study looking grim but sitting in a comfortable chair looking remarkably relaxed for someone who was supposedly cross with her.

'There you are, I have sent for coffee and pastries so we can be comfortable whilst we talk.'

He did not even comment on her disarray, the fact that she was still in her masculine garments with her hair in a tangle around her shoulders. Normally he would insist she changed before she appeared before him.

'That sounds quite delightful. Why have I been summoned?' It was obviously nothing untoward as otherwise he would not be smiling benevolently.

'Well, my dear, your mother and I have come up with the perfect solution to your reluctance to go to London. We are going to hold a house party here this summer and invite every eligible bachelor that we can find so that you may make a choice.'

'I have told you many times, Papa, that I have no wish to be leg-shackled. Surely you would prefer me to remain here and take care of you in your dotage? I promise I will be a devoted aunt to any children my brother might eventually produce with whoever he marries.'

'I shall not force you to take an offer that is unacceptable to you. I wish you to be happy, as happy as your mother and I have been these past years. There is the perfect partner for you somewhere, I am sure of it, we just have to find him. Tell me, sweetheart, what sort of man you want and I shall do my best to find him.'

Helena laughed. 'He must be tall, as tall as Theo at least. He must be handsome, rich, intelligent and kind.' She was warming to her theme now. 'All these traits are important, but what would be essential for me to accept a proposal is that the gentleman in question took me as I am. That he would not want me to conform, to behave as other young ladies do. Find me such a person and I give you my word I will marry him immediately.'

There was another most pertinent requirement but she thought it hardly suitable to mention to her parents. She would wish the marriage to be uncon-summated — a business arrangement between two friends.

'You do not require him to be in love with you, or you with him?' This question came from her mother.

'Not at all. I think respect and friendship are more important than romantic love.'

'The sort of gentleman you are describing, my dear, would be someone requiring your fortune. Would you be content to be married under those circumstances?'

'It would suit me very well. I should be able to continue my scientific studies whilst leaving him to spend my money as he wished.'

Her parents exchanged glances. 'In which case we shall set things in motion. As always, Helena, you must behave with decorum whilst there are guests here.'

'If I am to do that, Papa, then how shall I discover a gentleman who is not disgusted by my wearing such clothes as these, or spending my time with my head in a book, or locked away in my laboratory?'

'Shall we compromise, my dear? You will appear in your prettiest gowns on your best behaviour for the first few weeks. That should be time enough to sift through the gentlemen available. Only then will I give you permission to dress as you are now. Do you agree?'

She rushed across to embrace him. 'You are the best of fathers, it is small wonder that I do not wish to leave here because I cannot imagine being as happy anywhere else.'

After a pleasant hour discussing plans for the proposed house party, Helena escaped but was waylaid by her older brother, Theo, as he strode in through the front door.

'Good God, Sister, you are a disgrace to the family.' He opened his arms and she flew into them. He swung her around and she laughed.

'You will not believe what they have planned for me.' She quickly explained about the house party and he looked thoughtful.

'You might be hoisted by your own petard, my dear, and be forced to accept an offer this summer.'

'I hardly think so. There is not a gentleman in the land who would fit my stringent requirements.'

'You have not thought this through, Helena. You are the most beautiful and most eligible young lady in the county, if not the country. Do you really think someone would not pretend to acquiesce to your extraordinary demands in order to marry you? Once the knot is tied he would show his truc colours and there would be nothing any of us could do about it.'

She swallowed a lump in her throat. 'Then I shall rely on you to investigate all my suitors and not allow me to make such a disastrous error.'

He stretched out and removed several twigs from her hair. 'I shall just pray that you fall head over heels in love with one of the gentlemen and then you won't give a damn about any of your nonsensical requirements.'

'That will never happen. I am a woman of science. Such nonsense is for other young ladies, those with their heads full of the latest fashions and little else. You will stay here for the summer, will you not? I could not endure this house party without you at my side.'

'I would not miss it for the world, little sister. I am eager to find myself a bride and this would be an ideal opportunity. I shall suggest that an array of young ladies is invited too so we may both make a suitable choice.'

They strolled arm in arm to the drawing room where she left him to greet their parents. Her brother was five years her senior and there was no one else in this world she loved as much as him. It had been purgatory when he was away at school and she had lived for the holidays. Then he had gone up to Oxford and never returned to live with his family. He had his own

14

substantial estate an hour's ride from Faulkner Court, as well as managing joint business interests with their father.

'Are you intending to remain with us overnight or do you return to your home this evening, Theo?'

'I am staying until tomorrow morning. I trust you will appear in suitable raiment this evening? I am not accustomed to sitting down to dine with a young lady dressed in male attire.' Although this was said with due solemnity, his eyes were twinkling.

'I never dine like this, it would give poor mama palpitations. Papa only agreed to my being dressed as I am as long as I change for dinner.'

There was at least an hour before the gong would be rung and she had a pressing engagement in her laboratory. This was really a misnomer as it was merely the topmost room in a disused tower built by an earlier Faulkner. However, in this domain of hers she had glass bottles galore and a set of excellent lenses for viewing the items she had collected.

Her passion was scientific investigation, but she was also a talented artist and took great pleasure in recording her experiments for posterity. Already, she had amassed sufficient detailed illustrations of the flora and fauna of the area to make up a sizeable portfolio.

Her present obsession was to record in detail the opening of a flower, from the first small bud to the final fading glory of the seed pod. This meant that she had to be vigilant in order not to miss the slightest change.

After spending an hour in contented isolation, reluctantly she put down her pencils and watercolours and returned to the house. As always, she entered through a little-used side door and then scampered up the set of stairs that led to the guest chambers. As they rarely had guests, she was the only person to take this route. She scowled as she realised that when the house was full of unwanted visitors, not only would she be obliged to look and behave like a young lady, but would also have to abandon this staircase and use the handsome, ornately carved, oak stairs that dominated the entrance hall.

The following morning, she watched from her bedchamber as her brother left at first light. The only positive aspect of the proposed gathering was that he would be spending the entire summer at Faulkner Court.

Audley Manor, Hertfordshire.

Lord Christopher Drake, known to his friends and family as Kit, flung down his pen in despair. However hard he worked, however many corners he cut and economies he made, the two ends of his finances failed to meet.

Mama, bless her, had foregone the usual London seamstress for herself or the girls for the past two years and he no longer frequented Weston's or Hobbs for his jackets and his boots. If it hadn't been for the two trunks of

17

splendid Indian material that had been discovered in the attics, his three sisters and his mother would not have had new gowns at all.

The small estate he managed was not entailed, so he was free to sell off one of the farms — but in the current climate, and with the recently introduced Corn Laws, few gentlemen were prepared to risk their blunt on land. Mama had been hinting these past two years that there was one solution to their financial problems. He could marry money — not something he was eager to do.

Eloise, eight years his junior and the closest to him in age, had bravely offered to sacrifice herself on the marriage mart. He had dismissed this suggestion immediately. At just seventeen, she was far too young to be contemplating matrimony. No — he must bite the bullet and find himself the daughter of a wealthy cit who was looking for entry into the *ton*.

His title was hereditary. He believed that his grandfather might have been a duke, but when he'd asked his father about this possibility, his parent had been decidedly evasive. Whatever the truth of the matter was, he was a true aristocrat and could offer a future bride a place in society. Any progeny they might produce would be accepted into any drawing room in the country.

Too late to do anything about it this year; the Season was finishing and in the next few weeks the debutantes and hopeful bachelors would migrate to various country estates for the summer before it all began again next year.

Eloise would be eighteen and certainly considered old enough to parade at Almack's. She was petite, with golden curls and bright blue eyes — she would, despite her lack of dowry, be much in demand. He prayed she would not be forced to marry for pecuniary reasons but could marry a gentleman she loved. He would have to be wealthy, of course, but apart from that he would not object to a commoner.

Staring at the account ledgers would

not change the contents, so he might as well abandon the bookwork for today and take his new stallion for a gallop around the park. Lucifer, coal-black, had been produced at his own small stud and broken in by himself. Selling thoroughbreds was what had kept the family afloat these past few years. Lucifer would have to go in the autumn, but until then he would enjoy riding him.

Despite the fact that money was tight, he and his family went without, rather than his tenants and villagers. Every home in his demesne was watertight, every family well fed, and even those that were unemployed did not go hungry to bed. His father had been an excellent landlord too, as well as being a good husband, and excellent parent to him. It had been a sad blow to the family when he had succumbed to a congestion of the lungs a few months after Kit had reached his majority.

As always, he returned to the stables

in better spirits. As he was kicking his feet free of the irons, he was greeted by his dearest friend.

'Theo, what the devil are you doing here? Not that it isn't good to see you.'

'That's a handsome beast you have there, Kit. Is he perchance for sale?'

'He is. Are you interested?'

'I am indeed. I've had a long ride, I need to wash and change my clothes. Might I share the services of your valet as usual?'

'Of course. I take it you also intend to steal my clothes whilst you're here?'

His friend thumped him on the back. 'Do I not always do so? If the good Lord decided to make us of a similar build and height, then who are we to quibble?'

Kit was certain Theo hadn't come to purchase a horse. There was something else on his mind that had brought him here so unexpectedly. No doubt all would be revealed once his sisters and mother had retired and they could be private in his study.

2

Audley Manor, June 1810.

Kit could not help but notice Eloise was taking more interest in his friend than previously. Was it possible the two of them might make a match of it one day? There was nothing he would like better than to become part of Theo's family.

Eventually the ladies retired and he led the way to his sanctuary. No one, not even his mother, entered here unless by invitation. The evening was warm and he strolled to the far end and threw up the windows, letting in a cool breeze.

'It must be hideous in town at the moment, for those unfortunate enough to be attending a ball or some such nonsense.'

'I agree, so far I've managed to avoid

attending any functions during the Season. Which brings me nicely round to the purpose of my visit.'

'Brandy?' Kit waved an empty glass and his friend nodded. He poured them both a generous libation and folded his long length onto the chair opposite. 'Now, why are you here?'

'First, I must ask you a question. Are you still seriously considering marrying an heiress?'

'I am; why do you ask?'

'This might seem an extraordinary suggestion, but I think you should offer for my sister.'

Kit's drink slopped onto his knee and he swore. 'Good God, forgive me for saying so, my friend, but your sister would make the worst possible wife for any gentleman. She is wayward, wild and as unsuited to domesticity as any young lady in the country.'

Instead of being offended, his friend chuckled. 'Hear me out, Kit.'

By the time Theo had explained exactly what sort of husband his sister required, he was beginning to think there might be merit in his suggestion.

'The arrangement is to be in name only? I believe that until a union is consummated it's not considered legal.'

'Possibly not. How is this a concern to you? Unless either you or my sister wishes to have the marriage annulled, I cannot see that anyone would be aware of something so personal. The days of waving bloodstained sheets out of the window have long gone.'

'I would not enter into a union, even one as unusual as this, if I had any intention of setting it aside. There is one thing that might be a stumbling block — as you probably know, I keep a ladybird in a house in Kensington and have no intention of giving her up. If this was to be a true marriage, then obviously I would do so.'

'I hardly think this is a subject you will discuss with my sister, at least I hope not. She might be two and twenty, better read than any gentleman you might meet, and far more intelligent than I, but she's an innocent and has no knowledge whatsoever of such things.'

'I should hope not. If Helena is genuinely interested in a marriage of convenience, and more importantly, if your father is prepared to accept me as her husband, then I am prepared to speak to her.'

'No time like the present, old friend. I suggest you return with me tomorrow and get this matter sorted before the guests start arriving for the house party. I doubt there is anyone else who will fit her criteria so perfectly as yourself, but you never know.'

'Are my mother and sisters to receive an invitation?'

'Of course they are. There will be a dozen families, and although small children are excluded, there will be plenty of youngsters the same age as your sisters coming.'

'It is too long since we had anything to celebrate in this family. I had thought I would not be able to solve the financial crisis here until next spring. I cannot tell you what a relief it is to think that possibly, in a few weeks, I can pay the bills and be sure that my mother and sisters can continue to live comfortably.'

'Good God, man, I'm not sure either Helena or my parents will agree to such a precipitate arrangement. I had thought the autumn quite soon enough to tie the knot.'

'As long as we are formally betrothed and those that I owe money to are aware of it, then I am quite prepared to wait. However, if your sister wishes us to marry immediately then I shall be happy to do so. I hope that she understands that as far as the world's concerned she is my wife and must reside with me. She cannot remain at Faulkner Court.'

'You have a perfectly good carriage house that is not in use — if you are prepared to sacrifice it then it would make a perfect laboratory for her.'

'I shall discuss that with her myself.

Can I ask you not to mention my plans to my family? They must never know the true reason for my marriage. As far as they are concerned it will be a *coup de foudre*, a love match for both of us.'

Andover Hall, Hertfordshire.

The funeral of the Duke of Andover was a hurried and sad affair. The only mourners were the doctor, his lawyers and the new duke.

Richard had looked suitably miserable throughout the service and interment, but now he was in the privacy of his own home there was no need to dissemble.

'Your grace, there are some . . . some gentlemen asking to see you,' the butler said nervously.

'I have been expecting them, Potter. Have them brought to the study immediately. Have refreshments sent but then I have no wish to be disturbed. Is that quite clear?'

The man bowed. 'Yes, your grace. Will these gentlemen require bedchambers?'

'They will not. They will be leaving as soon as we have spoken.'

He walked somewhat unsteadily to the study that was now his. Perhaps it would be wise to cut down on the amount of alcohol he was consuming, at least until this business was settled.

The four men, ex-soldiers who had been recommended to him by a less-than-savoury crony, took the seats they were offered but refused either drink or food. This was a good sign. They were obviously professional men and would complete the task he was about to set them without difficulty. God knows, he was paying them a king's ransom so they ought to be efficient.

'There is someone I need disposing of. It must appear to be an accident. Is that something you can do?'

The man who had taken the central chair was obviously the leader. He nodded. His scarred face did nothing to improve his disreputable appearance. The other three were tough-looking characters. They were hard-eyed and thin-lipped — exactly what he wanted.

'We need the name of the individual, your grace. Half the money now and the rest on completion.'

'I have no notion of his actual whereabouts. I have written down what I do know about his parents and will leave the rest to you.'

One of the stipulations he had made in his search for assassins was that they would be literate, reasonably respectable, and not immediately recognisable as disreputable ruffians. They needed to be able to move about the countryside without attracting attention.

He handed over the paper with the scant information he had gleaned from the lawyers and then the large cloth bag stuffed full with money. Both vanished without being examined into an inside pocket in the leader's greatcoat.

The interview was over. The men

stood up, did not bow, but nodded as if to an equal and not someone of his status. They left without further conversation. Richard slumped into an armchair in front of the fire — even though the weather was clement, it was always damn cold in this barracks of a building. Once his succession was secure, he would raze it to the ground and build something modern, more suited to the nineteenth century than this monstrosity.

The lawyers were searching parish records, deeds and any other documentation they could find to discover the veracity of his father's dying words. Although he had laughed when he had heard the story, there was a ring of truth about it that he could not ignore.

The fact that this change of identities had supposedly taken place whilst the brothers had been up at Oxford made it more difficult. From what the legal crows had been able to tell him, his grandfather had promptly disowned the youngest son and he had left Andover and never been seen again.

One of them had told him there were several family properties scattered about the country that had belonged to Lord Drake and these had all been sold. They had yet to find out where the missing twin had settled. Something one of them had said as he left had done a lot to calm his nerves.

'Your grace, we only have the dying words of your father. I think it will be nigh on impossible to prove that the brothers exchanged places, as both of them are now deceased. It is possible, of course, that Lord Drake took documents with him to prove who he was, but until we find his family we cannot be sure.'

He wasn't going to take any chances. If there was the slightest possibility that his cousin was in fact the duke, he must be removed forthwith before the man married and produced another obstacle to the inheritance. The fact that he had just set in motion the murder of his closest relative bothered him not one jot. He could not do such a thing himself, but the death of someone he did not know was of no consequence to him.

He must observe the minimum period of mourning before he changed the way things were run here. He had no wish to bring unnecessary attention to his name until he was satisfied that the possible usurper was dead. Therefore, he would postpone any parties or extravagant expenditure until the six months was up. It was customary for a family to remain out of circulation for a year when a close member of the family died — six months would have to do in this case. No one would dare to question the behaviour of the Duke of Andover.

As the marquis, one would have expected to have been pursued by hopeful debutantes and their greedy mothers. However, his reputation as a rakehell, as a member of the most degenerate and disreputable gentlemen's clubs, had put off all but the most desperate. He was curious to see if, now that he was the duke, he would find himself more popular. As he had no intention of marrying, it would be a wasted effort on the part of any family who wished to ensnare him. As far as he was concerned, he would be the last of his line.

Faulkner Court

Helena shifted impatiently as the seamstress took her measurements. 'My lady, if you would be kind enough to remain still for a moment, I should be finished more quickly.'

'Helena, behave yourself. You will be free to rampage around the park as soon as you have selected the fabrics and styles for your new wardrobe.' Mama sighed noisily.

'I beg your pardon, dearest Mama, I shall be good. I must point out that I already have a closet full of gowns I've never worn so am at a loss to know why you think I need new ones.'

'My dear girl, I despair of you. You must be seen in the first stare of fashion — some of your gowns have the low waistline and others are in between. Today, fashion dictates that the waistline must be under your bosom.'

'Actually, I quite like this new style; it is far easier to move about without a corset.'

The shocked gasps from the two seamstresses and her mother made her laugh. 'Surely I am not expected to wear that restrictive garment under such a gown? My figure is slender, my waist quite small enough and my breasts firm without the need for whalebone to hold them up.'

If the listeners had been shocked before, now they were speechless at such bold talk from an unmarried young woman. Her mother recovered her composure.

'You will wear the necessary underpinnings, my girl, or I shall have you locked in your bedchamber.'

Helena smiled sweetly. 'As that is the outcome I desire then you have made my decision for me. If I'm to remain in my bedchamber for the duration of the house party then I do not have to make this ridiculous choice.'

She saw her mother's hands clench and for a moment thought a missile was going to be hurled in her direction, but Mama controlled her temper. With her customary elegance and grace, she rose to her feet and sailed out, her displeasure evident. Helena regretted her words. She loved both her parents and her brother unconditionally and did not deliberately set out to upset them.

The seamstress stepped away. 'I have finished, my lady. If you would care to make your selection from the patterns and pictures on the table before you leave?' The remainder of the sentence was left unsaid but Helena knew if she stormed out now it was unlikely this prestigious mantua-maker would agree to make the journey from London a second time.

She flicked through the fashion plates and put half a dozen to one side. She gave the material samples more attention and selected none of the insipid pastel colours a debutante would be expected to wear.

'I apologise for my ill humour. I know colours are not usual for an unmarried lady, but I am well past the age of a debutante. I have been out for years, so if I must have new gowns then I shall have them in colours and styles that would suit me.'

'I think everything you have selected, my lady, will be perfect. I can see no objection to you having a ballgown in emerald green as it exactly matches the colour of your eyes. Also, avoiding yellows, oranges and pinks is sensible with your beautiful russet hair.'

'Thank you, I do not deserve your praise. Can I leave you to select the necessary bonnets, gloves, reticules, stockings and so on that I shall need to complete my ensembles?'

The woman curtsied. 'I should be honoured to do so, my lady. I shall have the first of your day gowns, and an evening gown, sent to you by the end of the week. The remainder of your wardrobe will be delivered as it is completed. You are fortunate that my workshop isn't busy at this time of the year.'

Mary, her personal dresser, had her usual garb of specially made breeches, shirt, waistcoat and jacket waiting on the bed. 'I wish to put on a gown, something pretty that my mother would approve of.'

Within a quarter of an hour, she was dressed in forget-me-not blue muslin with a pretty scalloped neckline and a darker blue ribbon tied under her bosom. Helena hurried off in search of her mother so she could make a grovelling apology for her earlier immodest comments and unruly behaviour.

The sound of voices led her to the drawing room where her parents were having a lively discussion — no doubt about herself. Mama did her best but Papa was indulgent and Helena knew herself to be thoroughly spoiled.

'Mama, I have come to say I am sorry and that I will do better in future. You do not deserve to have such a wild daughter as myself.'

'Silly girl, I cannot be cross with you for more than a few moments. You look beautiful in that gown. I appreciate the effort you have made on my behalf. Come and sit with us and we shall tell you what we are planning for your house party.'

When they had finished, she was for the first time in her life lost for words. 'Stilt-walkers, fire-eaters, fortune tellers, as well as country picnics, visits to historic sites and charades, dinner parties and dances? I have never been so excited in my life. Thank you so much for doing this.' She tilted her head to one side and fluttered her eyelashes at her besotted father. 'Papa, I promise I shall enjoy every moment and do my very best to find myself a suitable husband.'

'That is all that we ask of you, my love. To tell you the truth, I am as excited as you are at the prospect of so much occurring here. Is there anything else you would like us to add to the list of entertainment?'

'There is one thing — could we have excursions on horseback as well as drives in carriages?'

'It will be added to the list immediately. I thank the good Lord we are holding this event in the summer so the horses can be turned out, as we do not have the stabling for so many.'

3

Faulkner Court

Helena wandered to the window whilst her papa continued to talk to her.

'Remember always, my dear girl, that the choice must be yours. There will be nobody coming to the house party that your mama and I have not already decided would make you a suitable partner. Therefore, if a gentleman does offer for you then you can be sure he will have my full approval.'

'Good heavens! I do believe it is Theo cantering up the drive, and he has a companion with him. Are we expecting an early guest?' Helena pressed her nose to the glass and peered out like an urchin. 'It's Kit. I wonder why he has come today and not waited to come with his mama and sisters.'

She waved vigorously and both riders

raised their whips in acknowledgement. She was too far away to see the expressions on their faces but she could be sure they would both be looking disapproving because of her behaviour.

'Thank goodness you are dressed correctly today, my love. I believe that the last time Lord Drake was here, he spent the entire time looking for caterpillars in the oak tree.'

'Has he not been here since then? That's almost a year ago. I am fond of Kit — no, do not look hopeful, Mama, he's far too like Theo to make me a good husband. I need a compliant gentleman, not someone as dictatorial and formidable as my brother.'

'I suggest that you sit down and practice being a well-behaved young lady and not a hoyden. Having Kit here early is fortuitous as you can flirt with him without fear he will fall head over heels in love with you.'

'Mama, what fustian you talk! He is as likely to fall in love with me as I am to fly to the moon. He thoroughly disapproves of me and my choice of lifestyle and has said so on numerous occasions . . . '

Her mother smiled in that particular way she had when she knew something that her daughter did not. 'My love, I think you must be the only person in the county who does not realise just how beautiful you are. I own that I am biased, but I am confident there will be no other young ladies present this summer who will outshine you.'

'It's not the outside of a person that counts, as far as I'm concerned, but what's inside.'

'Now who is talking fustian? One of your firm stipulations about the gentleman you wish to marry was that he was personable and not only that, that he was more than two yards high and broad in the shoulders.' Mama was correct to point this out.

She remained at the window watching her brother and his best friend approach. She had already been seen gawping at them so there was no point pretending she hadn't. They were now close enough for her to look more closely at her brother's companion.

Apart from his tendency to give her a bear-garden jaw, to expect her to follow his commands to the letter, he fitted exactly her criteria. Was it possible that she had had him in mind all along?

She walked out to stand on the steps beneath the portico to greet them as they arrived. Word had already been sent around to the stable and two lads were there to take their reins and lead the sweating horses away.

'Theo, Kit, to what do we owe this unexpected pleasure?' This was not what she had intended to say but, as usual, she spoke what she was thinking and it was too late to repine.

Instead of looking annoyed at her impertinence, Kit was looking at her strangely, as if he'd never seen her before. His eyes were blue, so dark they were almost black, and they had an intensity about them that was unnerving. Her cheeks coloured and she shifted from one foot to the other.

Her brother stepped between her and his friend, breaking the eye contact and setting her free to move. 'That is a remarkably pretty ensemble, Sister, I scarcely recognised you.'

'Thank you, Brother. You have not answered my question as to why you've returned so soon — after all, you only departed yesterday morning and yet here you are again today.'

'Kit wishes to speak to you and it couldn't wait.'

Something she didn't recognise almost made her knees buckle. Was she going down with a summer fever? She knew exactly what Lord Drake had come to do — he'd come to make her an offer and the notion quite terrified her.

'I have a megrim coming. Excuse me, I must go and lie down. I shall not join you for dinner.' She gathered her skirts and fled, but Kit was somehow in front of her, blocking the passage.

'Please, sweetheart, do not run away

from me. We are friends, are we not? I have a proposition to make to you and all I ask is that you listen.'

She wanted to refuse but there was something in his eyes that made her nod. She could not do more than that, as her words were somehow stuck in her throat. When he placed his gloved hand on the small of her back, it made her jump. It also returned the power of speech to her.

'Kindly remove your hand from my person, Lord Drake.' Her voice was commendably steady despite the pounding of her heart.

Instantly he did as she asked, but his eyes narrowed and she knew in that moment that whatever he said, however persuasive he was, she would not accept his offer.

'We can use the library, my lord. It is cool in there and we shall not be disturbed.'

She stalked ahead of him, her hands clenched at her sides, praying she would not collapse at his feet like a silly child. There was a small bureau, flanked by chairs, at the far end of the room in front of the window. She walked there and sat down. He took the chair opposite. The only sound was that of the birds outside and the loud ticking of the longcase clock. She was surprised he couldn't hear her heart pounding.

'I know what you wish to say. My brother has told you I am looking for a husband and he told me you are looking for a rich wife.'

Her bluntness did not improve the chilly atmosphere. She waited for him to comment but he was ominously silent.

'If Theo told you about my plans then he will have told you that I will only marry if I can find a gentleman who fulfils each one of my criteria. We both know that you do not.'

He leaned back in the chair and crossed his arms before speaking. 'I am not a vain man, but neither am I blind. I know that I more than fit your physical requirements for a husband. I am also certain that I have all the other attributes you want. Therefore, I am at a loss to know why you have rejected me before you've heard what I have to say.'

He sounded genuinely interested in her reply. This emboldened her to speak truthfully, not that she ever did anything else.

'I agree that you have all the things you mention, but what you don't have is more important than what you do. I have no intention of giving up my scientific experiments, of moderating my wild behaviour, and neither do I wish to attend supper parties, soirees or balls, or stand as hostess to similar events in my own house.'

'Do go on, my lady, I am riveted by your expectations.'

'Also, the gentleman that I marry will agree for it to be in name only. I dislike physical contact of any sort.'

He smiled politely and raised an aristocratic eyebrow. 'Is that it? Are you quite sure there is nothing else you wish to add to your extraordinary list?'

She didn't quite like the look on his face and wished she had been less forceful in her words and showed him a little more respect. 'I believe I have made myself perfectly clear, my lord. I think you must also understand why you are the last person I would consider as a suitable candidate for my hand.'

'I shall be as frank as you, my dear. I can assure you that if I was not in desperate financial need I would not contemplate for a moment offering to marry you. You are the very last young woman on the planet that I would ask under normal circumstances.' She thought this comment harsh but decided it might be wiser to hold her tongue for the moment.

'I have my mother and sisters' welfare to consider, otherwise I would not be here. I will give you my word as a gentleman that I agree to abide by every one of the requirements on your list. However, I have some prerequisites of my own that you must agree to before this can go further.'

All she could do was nod; she was too shocked to speak.

'You may dress as you please, ride astride, continue with your ridiculous experiments as long as we are at Audley Manor and we are not entertaining. You will have separate quarters and may bring your own retainers. My mother will remain mistress of the house.'

'I cannot cavil at your demands, my lord. I can hardly expect to be your chatelaine if I'm not prepared to take on the usual obligations of a wife.' There was a look of satisfaction on his face that she disliked. Otherwise, she would never have said what she did.

★ ★ ★

Kit had decided in an instant that he was going to marry Helena — not because he needed the money but because he had seen her clearly for the first time. How could he have been so blind all these years? Her unruly behaviour and outlandish dress had made him see her not as she really was, but as an aberration, a young lady to be avoided at all costs.

The fact that she was wearing a delightful gown had shown him just how beautiful she was, but that wasn't why he had fallen irrevocably in love with her. The fact that he had come here to make her an offer had somehow drawn back the curtains that had obscured the girl from his sight. He had every intention of making her his true wife but would keep to his word until he persuaded her to fall in love with him.

He was going to enjoy the next few months. Not only was his family going to be financially secure, he now had the challenge of showing this wonderful girl what it was to be a woman. For all her outward maturity, she was still a child in many respects. She had grown up adored and spoilt by the entire family, had never been disciplined, and had been allowed to go her own way until now.

Then she said something so shocking, he was forced to reconsider his assessment of her character.

'I shall not object to you keeping your mistress in London, my lord. I could hardly ask a virile man like yourself to remain celibate.'

He jerked forward so violently his elbows slammed against the edge of the table. The pain made him swear. 'God dammit to hell!' He surged to his feet and saw her recoil in her chair but he was too angry to hold back his words. 'How dare you mention such a thing to me?' He was almost incapable of continuing and leaned forward so his face was inches from hers.

'I thought you an innocent but am obviously sadly mistaken.' He hadn't intended to accuse her of being impure but the words had just come out of their own volition.

Her fear changed instantly to anger. She pushed herself upright so violently the top of her head caught him under the chin and his jaws snapped shut so hard he bit through his tongue.

He reeled backwards, his mouth full of the metallic taste of blood, clapping his hands to his mouth to stem the flow. When he recovered his balance, she appeared to have gone, but then to his horror he saw her spread-eagled on the boards, unconscious.

He groped in his pocket, found his handkerchief and held it over his mouth. There was nothing he could do for Helena whilst he was almost choking on his own gore. In two strides he reached the bell-strap and pulled it. His head was spinning. If he did not sit, he was likely to join the girl on the floor.

The library door had been left open and a footman stepped in. There was no need for Kit to explain, even if he had been able to speak. He put his head down between his knees. Better the blood flowed forward, away from his lungs, however gruesome it might look.

The sound of pounding feet

approaching told him help was at hand. Theo burst in. 'Good God! What has taken place here?'

Kit was unable to speak: his tongue had swollen, making this impossible, and only by breathing through his nose was he able to remain conscious himself. He thought the bleeding had stopped and he attempted to spit out what was in his mouth.

'Let me see. Open your mouth.'

He tried to do as Theo instructed but his enlarged tongue made this difficult. He didn't raise his head, breathing was easier with it lowered.

'I see what has happened. The gash on your tongue has closed, but you will have to remain as you are for the present. I did the same thing when I came off my pony as a boy: horribly painful, but the swelling went down within an hour so I could breathe normally again.'

Kit raised his hand to indicate he understood and then gestured towards Helena.

'She has come round; she has a large bump on the top of her head, and will be escorted to her bedchamber. You came off worst from this encounter, my friend.'

Then she was beside him. 'I am so sorry, this is all my fault, Kit. I should not have said something so appalling.'

He could not apologise for what he'd said and it was far worse than her immodest statement. Instead he held out his hand and she clasped it between hers.

'When you are better, I shall come and speak to you.'

She released him and he would have smiled, had he been able to. She refused any offer of assistance and insisted she was quite capable of getting to her chamber unaided. He glanced down, shocked to see the hand he had offered her was red. He could think of no other young lady, even his sisters, who would have held his hand the way it was.

'Up you come, old fellow, we shall

help you to the *chaise longue*. Don't raise your head, we will guide you.'

Once he was safely seated again, he leaned back gratefully and lifted his legs so they were on the daybed too. Someone covered him with a rug, and he closed his eyes and let his mind drift away.

How could he have been so crass as to accuse Helena of being impure? He had behaved badly and did not deserve her forgiveness. He considered himself a peaceable sort of fellow, one who avoided violence of any kind — even verbal. He expected his wishes to be obeyed, to be treated with the respect he was due, but until today he had never lost his temper.

His tongue throbbed unpleasantly but he believed the swelling was abating, as he could now breathe more easily. He doubted he would be able to talk coherently for a considerable time; he felt as if his mouth was full of a wet facecloth.

He dozed for a while, until there was

the rattle of a tray beside him. 'Kit, you need to drink to replace the blood you lost. Mama insists it should be watered wine, so I have some here.'

Obediently, he held out his hand and a glass was put in it. Swallowing was difficult and most of the liquid dribbled down his chin. He wiped it away with his shirtsleeve before his friend could offer to do it for him.

When had his topcoat been removed? He didn't recall that happening. He wriggled his toes — his boots had gone too. He must have passed out for a while.

He had another attempt at drinking and this time was more successful. When he had downed three brimming glasses, he held up his hand to indicate he'd had enough, and then swung his stockinged feet to the ground.

'Lean on me, Kit, I'll help you up to your room. My sister has retired. You will be able to see her tomorrow when you can speak again.'

The wine on an empty stomach had

gone to his head. He was relieved to reach his apartment without collapsing in a drunken stupor. That would just add to his humiliation. Theo didn't ask how the accident had happened; presumably, his sister had explained.

The young man who always acted as his valet when he was at Faulkner Court was waiting to help him undress. The fact that he and his friend were identical in size and had similar taste, meant that neither of them bothered to take garments with them when they visited. They borrowed from each other's wardrobes.

Kit fell into bed and was instantly asleep. He awoke some hours later and was pleased to find his tongue, although sore, had now returned to its normal size. He could open and shut his mouth and was certain he could talk. More to the point, he was ravenously hungry.

There was sufficient moonlight filtering in through the closed shutters for him to see to scramble out of bed. He dragged on the night-robe hanging over the end of the bed and headed for the door. The sconces were left alight in the passageways, so he should be able to find his way to the kitchen without difficulty.

4

Helena had her abigail draw the curtains around her bed and then the girl was sent away and told not to come unless called for. Apart from an unpleasant ache in the region that had the lump on it, she was perfectly well. What she wasn't, was happy about her part in the accident.

Kit would never infer she was anything but an innocent; she had misinterpreted his words and caused him serious damage. There had been so much blood, his topcoat and shirt were quite covered in it, and despite being assured he was recovering rapidly she was not sanguine that this was the true case.

She was unable to sleep. She tossed and turned and eventually the house was quiet. Now she could venture forth and see for herself that he was recovered. Then she would go down to the kitchen and find herself something to eat. She had a healthy appetite and after missing her dinner, she was sharp-set and could not possibly survive the night without finding something substantial to fill the space.

There was no need for her to dress, the nightgown she was wearing covered her from head to toe without revealing an inch of her flesh. With her bedrobe over the top, she could be seen by anyone without fear of embarrassment.

Kit was considered part of the family, so was on this side of the house. She swayed and was obliged to put out a hand to keep herself upright. Was he about to become an actual member of her family in the near future? He was as far from her mental picture of a compliant husband as chalk was from cheese but . . . but she already loved him as a brother, so wouldn't he make the perfect person for her to marry?

She pushed these confusing thoughts to the back of her head and headed for the chamber he always used. Her stomach rumbled loudly. No — she would eat first and investigate the patient second. As he didn't know she was about to visit him, he would not consider her tardy when she did not appear until later.

It was not the first nocturnal visit she had made to the kitchens, and the servants' domain downstairs was familiar to her. From a small child, she had been welcome there; her parents had not objected as they did not stand on ceremony at Faulkner Court.

The wall sconces burned brightly upstairs but were doused downstairs, so she would need to find herself a candle. As the weather was so warm, there were no fires lit anywhere and she would have to push a candle into a wall sconce in order to light it.

This was also something she had done on more than one occasion. Obviously, the sconces in the reception rooms were out; only the passageways remained illuminated. She found a candle and carried a chair from the dining room so she had something to stand on.

She was in the process of gathering her skirts to jump onto the chair when Kit strolled up beside her. 'Allow me, sweetheart, I can reach without the necessity of using that chair.' He removed the candle from her unresisting fingers and then solemnly handed it back to her once it was burning.

'You look unhurt, how can that be when there was so much blood and you were gasping for breath a few hours ago?'

His smile was warm. He obviously held no animosity towards her for injuring him so grievously. 'It looked far worse than it was. I am, as I presume you are, on my way to the kitchen. I cannot tell you how glad I am to see you, as I think I shall get a better repast with you at my side.'

'As you have surmised, I have done this many times before. The only punishment I ever received, however appalling my behaviour, was to be sent to bed without supper. Needless to say, on those occasions I did not remain hungry for long.'

'You are incorrigible, sweetheart, and horribly spoilt.'

She held her breath, waiting for him to continue this comment by saying he would take her in hand once they were married, but he said no more on the subject.

'I intend to have coffee so need to attend to the range.' She happened to glance down and saw his long, lean feet beneath his night garments. 'You have no slippers on, Kit. Sit down at once and remove your feet from the flag-stones. I have no wish to be the cause of you catching a congestion of the lungs.'

His deep, baritone laughter echoed around the empty room. 'I can assure you I shall suffer no ill health from walking about on bare feet. However, I shall do as you ask as I have no wish to hinder your preparation of our mid-night feast.'

'I assume that you know how to make coffee?' He nodded. 'Good, then you can do that whilst I do everything else. I shall get what you need and put it on the table.'

She found venison pie, slices of succulent, homegrown ham, half a loaf of bread and a jar of cook's excellent chutney. All she needed now was butter and something sweet for afterwards. There was half an apple pie and a jug of cream that would be perfect for dessert.

She took the laden tray into the kitchen and put it on the table. She was astonished to see he had found the necessary cutlery and crockery and had laid it out for them. There was also a steaming jug of her favourite beverage waiting.

Her stomach gurgled for a second time and she giggled. 'I apologise, my lord, but as you can hear, I am in need of this food.'

'Then let us eat.'

She heaped a selection of items on each plate and set to with gusto. She had been munching contentedly for a few minutes when she became aware that he wasn't eating.

He smiled ruefully. 'Despite my desire to eat this delicious repast, I find that I cannot chew. No, don't look so unhappy. I shall not starve if I cannot eat for a day or two. I can drink as long as it is not too hot.'

She dropped her cutlery with a clatter and was on her feet immediately. 'There is soup in the pantry. It will not take but a moment for me to heat you some.'

Not waiting for his response she rushed off and came back with a tureen of soup. He was watching her without comment and she found this unnerving. Soon, the contents of the saucepan were steaming and she tipped it into the waiting bowl.

'There you are, it's warm, so should be perfect.'

He picked up his spoon and ladled some into his mouth. She held her breath to see if he managed to swallow.

His glance flicked up to her. 'My dear, if I am to dribble this down my chin I would prefer it if you were not watching.'

'I beg your pardon. I shall return to my own supper. I can assure you that I am enjoying every mouthful and have no intention of dribbling it anywhere.'

To her consternation he reached across the table and rapped her smartly on the knuckles with his spoon. The fact that it had recently been in his mouth made this even more astonishing.

'That was uncalled for, my lord, I am the epitome of helpfulness and do not deserve to be physically chastised.' She risked a peep at him. His eyes were glimmering with amusement but he continued to consume the soup without comment.

Without being asked, she refilled the saucepan and once it was warm, tipped it into his empty bowl. She then resumed her seat and made inroads into the apple pie and cream. When she was replete she wiped her sticky fingers and mouth on her napkin and poured herself a cup of coffee.

'I could make you some junket, that's sloppy and soft . . . '

His hand moved like lightning and she received a second sharp tap from his spoon. This was the outside of enough and she was not going to sit quietly and ignore his abuse this time. She was still holding her full cup and she tipped it over his hands. She had been tempted to throw it in his face, but thought that might have been doing it too brown.

Helena gripped the edge of the table, poised to throw herself backwards if he retaliated in kind. Instead, he laughed.

'I think we can call the contest even, my dear. Shall I pour you another cup, as I am quite certain this one will be drunk and not thrown?' Although his tone was light, she detected the warning and heeded it.

'Thank you, that would be absolutely splendid.' She waited until her cup was full and then drained it. 'I am returning to my apartment. I bid you good night. No doubt we shall speak again tomorrow.'

'Sit down, sweetheart, I wish to conclude the conversation we started earlier.'

Reluctantly she did as she was bid and sat, looking down, hands folded in her lap, pretending to be a demure and docile young lady.

'Look at me. I have no intention of speaking to the top of your head.'

Again, she obeyed his instruction. He had pushed the used crockery and cutlery to one side and was leaning forward. His elbows were on the table with his hands supporting his head.

'I offer you my unreserved apology, Helena. I behaved disgracefully and I give you my word I shall not . . . '

'Please, Kit, do not make promises you will not be able to keep.' His expression of incredulity made her smile. He sat up straight and regarded her as if she were a candidate for a lunatic asylum. 'If we are to proceed with this business arrangement then I can guarantee I shall force you to lose your temper on a regular basis. Ask Theo, he will tell you I am the most annoying and infuriating of young ladies.'

'You still wish to marry me if I accept your terms?'

'I do. I also owe you an apology for mentioning your mistress ... ' She wished the words unspoken as his expression changed from friendly to formidable. She refused to be cowed by his anger or his size. If this arrangement was to work, she could not allow herself to be intimidated. 'Do not scowl at me, sir, I am not one of your sisters, to be frightened into silence.'

His shoulders relaxed but he was no longer amused. 'Then pray, continue. I am agog to know what outrageous thing you intend to say next.'

'I would like you to know that I shall not take a lover, as I would never bring a bastard into your nursery.'

His mouth dropped open and, for a second, he looked like a fish gasping for breath on the bank after it had been landed. Only then did she notice that his knuckles were white. The fact that he was gripping the table so hard gave her pause. Should she not have used the word *bastard?*

'I apologise if my language has offended . . . '

'Be quiet. If you say another word I shall not be answerable for the consequences. Remove yourself from my sight, before I reconsider my response.'

There were times when one could stay and reason with the person you had inadvertently offended, but she had the sense to understand that this was not one of them. Despite her fear, she stood up slowly, but did not run away as he expected.

She nodded, and without another word, sailed from the kitchen with her head held high. As soon as she was a few yards away from him, she took to her heels, fled to her apartment and flung herself in. She was at a loss to know why he had been so angry with her. If they were to have a business arrangement, if he was to continue to visit his mistress, surely she might have expected to have the same privileges as he?

She hadn't been exactly sure what the marital act entailed until her parents had started talking about her attending the next Season. She had known that sharing a bed with a man would likely as not result in an infant nine months later, but was ignorant of how this miracle took place. When she had enquired from her mother, she had been told everything would be explained to her before she married, but until then young ladies should not ask such questions.

Mary, her maid, had initially been equally reluctant to discuss the matter, although Helena was quite certain the girl knew all the details. When Helena had insisted, what she had been told was so horrifying she thought it could not possibly be true. She shivered when she remembered the conversation.

'You've seen animals mating in the farmyard, haven't you, my lady?'

'Of course I have, what has that to do with it?'

'Everything. It's the same for people as it is for beasts.'

Mary had said no more and from that moment on, Helena had been determined that she would never put herself in such an undignified position. If this meant that she would never marry, then so be it. Up until that point, she had been unconventional, but not as outrageous and wild as she was now. This had been a deliberate ploy on her part to ensure no local gentlemen tried to persuade her to marry him.

Refusing to go to London was not because she was that averse to parties, pretty gowns or attending a ball, but because she was terrified of falling in love, accepting an offer, and then having to endure what came next.

She had only mentioned that she had no intention of taking a lover because she wished Kit to understand that she was a woman-grown, not a child, and expected to be treated with respect.

★ ★ ★

Kit had recovered from his anger before she reached the door but decided to let her go. If this was how they dealt together then marrying her would be dangerous for both of them. What was it about her that stirred his senses? He had spent many hours in her company and had never once been cross with her and yet, in the space of a few hours, he had lost his temper twice and had just realised he had been in love with her for years.

He was equally determined that whatever the risks or pitfalls, he would marry her. Not because she was an heiress but because no other young lady would do. He could never love another as he did her. Things had been simpler when he had not had feelings for her — in fact, being in love just complicated matters. He decided that his irascible humour was a direct result of the fact that what he really wanted to do was take her in his arms and kiss her breathless.

He surveyed the ruins of the table and decided he would remove the evidence of their visit. Why give the servants more reason to gossip about their betters? By the time the task was done, he was regretting not having put on his slippers before coming down.

Helena had taken the candlestick but he thought he could find his way easily enough in the dark. He was almost as familiar with this house as he was his own, having spent so much time here over the past few years. He and Theo had been firm friends; they had met at school and often spent holidays in each other's company. The fact that he was two years younger than his friend had never been a barrier to them.

He heard the clock in the entrance

hall strike two, it would be light soon. As he was passing her door, he noticed a sliver of light under it and some impulse drove him to knock softly. If she did not reply, he would continue to his own chamber.

The door opened. 'Come in, we need to talk.'

She pointed to a chair by the window and then took one as far away as was possible in her sitting room. He sat and waited silently for her to begin the conversation.

'I don't understand why we have been constantly at daggers drawn today. We were always the best of friends up until now — what has changed? Despite the fact that you are the ideal candidate, I cannot marry you if you are going to lose your temper at the slightest thing.'

'It is indeed, sweetheart, a conundrum. I think the explanation is quite simple. Until a few hours ago, we viewed each other as siblings and now we are forced to consider the possibility that we will be life partners.' She was watching him closely and he knew he must choose his next words carefully. 'Remember, you told me not to promise something I could not adhere to. You will continue to infuriate me and I shall continue to lose my temper. I do not see that as an obstacle. I think it will make our arrangement more interesting. Do you not agree?'

'I am not sure that being shouted at and terrified by your fury could be described as interesting. However, our partnership will certainly not be dull. If I thought you would do more than castigate me verbally I could not possibly continue with this, but I am certain you will never hurt me physically, however appalling my behaviour.'

He felt a stab of guilt at her trust. He wasn't sure he would not wish to toss her across his knee at some point in the future. 'You are quite correct to say that I would never strike a child or a woman, whatever the circumstances.'

Her smile made his stomach clench.

What was going to be far harder was keeping the relationship platonic.

'I have given the matter due consideration and I have decided to accept your offer and your conditions, as you have already agreed to accept mine.'

He returned her smile and her cheeks coloured. 'I'm not aware that I have made you a formal offer, my lady. I shall do so now.'

Her eyes widened as he dropped to one knee before her. 'Lady Helena, will you do me the inestimable honour of becoming my wife?' He clutched his chest in a parody of romantic love.

She responded in kind. 'La, my lord, I am quite overcome by your kind offer.' She clasped her hands and fluttered her eyelashes, not knowing that even her play-acting was having a disastrous effect on his control. 'I believe that I will accept you.'

He rose smoothly to his feet and reached out and gently pinched her cheek, a gesture more appropriate from an uncle to a niece. 'Then we are betrothed. I shall speak to your father tomorrow. No doubt you require several months to prepare your bride clothes and so on.'

'I do not. In fact, the house party can now be cancelled as its sole purpose was for me to select a husband.' Then she shook her head. 'Would you mind very much if we still held it? My parents have gone to so much trouble and you will not believe the entertainment they have arranged for everyone.'

'Sweetheart, it is not my decision to make. As long as all the eligible gentlemen are aware that you are spoken for then I see no reason for it to be cancelled. Do you mean that you wish to be married soon?'

'If the banns are called this Sunday then we could be married before the house party is finished — that means we have no need to invite guests as they will already be here.'

It was difficult not to show his delight at her suggestion. He had no wish to frighten her off by his enthusiasm. 'I do not want to rush you into anything, but I am happy to go along with your idea. Where would you like to go for our wedding trip?'

'I had not thought that far ahead. I have never travelled anywhere apart from London. I would dearly like to visit Derbyshire and the Lake District and perhaps even go to Scotland.'

'Then I shall make arrangements for us to travel north. Shall we ride or do you wish to travel in a carriage?'

She looked at him as if he was speaking in tongues. 'Ride hundreds of miles? We would need a string of horses to do that.'

'Not at all. If we travel slowly, both the horses and ourselves will enjoy the journey. My man of affairs, Duncan, who is also my valet, and your maid, can travel separately with our luggage and make arrangements for our overnight stops.'

Before he could prevent it, she flew across the room and flung herself into his arms. Feeling her pressed close to him was almost his undoing. He patted her briskly on the back and then stepped out of her embrace.

'I am glad that I can please you so easily, Helena. It will be my pleasure to show you the countryside. We have no reason to hurry, as we have the best part of four months before the weather becomes inclement.'

'I had not thought giving up my independence could be so exciting. Kit, you must return to your apartment. It would not do for anyone to find you here and both of us in our nightclothes.'

'Indeed, it would not. Good night, Helena.'

He left her as happy as a schoolgirl before a party. His smile was rueful. To him, she must remain just that, if he was going to be able to stick to his side of the bargain.

5

This time, when Helena returned to bed, she was asleep the moment her head touched the pillow. Usually she was up with the lark, but the next morning she didn't stir until Mary came in with her morning chocolate and sweet rolls.

'What do you wish me to put out for you today, my lady?'

'Something elegant, I have no wish to look like a hoyden.'

Her morning ablutions took longer than usual, as did the dressing of her hair and the arranging of her ensemble. She viewed herself in the full-length glass and was satisfied with what she saw. With her hair arranged on top of her head, a few curls allowed to drift down on either side of her face, she thought she looked almost grown-up.

The gown her maid had chosen for

her was in the fashionable style: sprigged muslin in pale green, with dark green flowers embroidered around the hem, neckline and sleeves. She hitched up the front. There was far too much of her bosom showing, in her opinion. 'I think I should have a fichu, I am sure we have one somewhere to tuck in here.'

'No, my lady, that gown is perfect as it is. Will you be riding later?'

'I hope so. Please leave out my habit and boots. There's no need for you to be here to help me change, I am perfectly capable of doing that myself.'

The girl curtsied. 'Thank you, my lady, I have a deal of mending to do and would be grateful for the time to do that.'

Was Kit up? Would he speak to her papa before they broke their fast or leave it until later? She did not have long to wait to discover the answer. Her mother was waiting for her in the entrance hall.

'Mama, how are you up so early? Is Papa up also?'

'I have no idea, my love. Kit came to see me and explained what you have decided, so I had to get up to speak to you. My dear girl, you have made the perfect choice and I am absolutely delighted. Kit has said you want to be married immediately. Are you quite sure you do not wish to wait until the autumn? Have time to adjust to what will be very different circumstances?'

Helena was about to tell her mother the reason for her eagerness but then thought better of it. One thing she was quite sure about was that neither parent would approve of Kit's plans. Travelling in a carriage was what a sensible young lady did — she should not be gallivanting about the country on a horse.

She quickly explained why she thought holding the ceremony during the house party made sense and her mother nodded.

'I am content for it to go ahead as soon as the banns have been read. I have decided there will be a celebratory ball in the evening of your nuptials and to that will be invited any neighbours and friends who are not attending the house party.'

'I hope that some of my new gowns shall be ready by then. There is one I particularly liked and I think it will be perfect for my wedding day.'

'There are four weeks before the day — ample time for the seamstress to complete everything you ordered.' Her mother slipped her arm through hers and in perfect harmony they strolled to the breakfast parlour. As soon as she stepped in, her brother snatched her up and swung her around.

'Well done, little sister, I am delighted that Kit will now be a member of this family and I can call him brother.'

'Thank you, Theo, I know I have made the right choice.' Only then did she realise her future husband was standing by the breakfast buffet listening to every word that was said.

His smile was friendly, no different from any other he had ever bestowed upon her. 'We will make a good team, Helena. I know that my mother and sisters will be equally pleased at our betrothal.'

She glided up beside him and picked up a plate. 'You have not mentioned our wedding trip arrangements, have you? I don't think my papa would approve.'

He winked. 'I am not a nodkin, sweetheart. As far as they are concerned we shall be going directly to Audley Manor.'

'They will think that poor of you, not to take me on a trip. Perhaps we could tell them we are going to spend a week or two in Bath?'

His grimace made her giggle. 'I would rather have my teeth pulled than go there. However, I shall do as you suggest, as I have no wish to put any obstacles in the way of the arrangements by upsetting your parents.'

Satisfied with his response, she piled her plate high and took it to the table. He sat next to her and then her brother joined them. Her father rarely ate breakfast and her mother usually had hers sent to her room. How had Mama been up so early this morning? They munched in companionable silence for a bit.

'I shall be riding later,' she announced, her voice overloud. Both gentlemen looked at her. Their scrutiny made her uncomfortable and she could think of nothing further to say on the subject.

'Thank you for telling us. I shall be in the study with your father, arranging the settlement.' Kit looked expectantly at Theo.

'I'm damned if I know what I'll be doing. I might ride with you, Helena.'

They returned to concentrating on their food. This quite ridiculous. The three of them were talking as if they were complete strangers. Why should the fact that she was going to marry her brother's best friend makes things so stilted?

She put down her cutlery and banged the table loudly with her fist. Kit's hand jerked so violently, a piece of ham he had speared on the end of his fork flew across the table, landing squarely on her brother's grey silk waistcoat. Theo had been pouring coffee and a circle of brown liquid marred the white tablecloth. He had also somehow managed to cover his jacket sleeve as well.

She had certainly got their undivided attention now.

'Have you taken leave of your senses, Sister?' Her brother said as he peeled the ham from his person.

'Good God! I am about to marry a lunatic.'

She tried to suppress the inappropriate desire to laugh at their outrage, but was unsuccessful. Her attempt to hide her giggles behind her napkin failed dismally. She was snorting and hiccupping in a most unladylike manner.

Kit pulled her hands from her face and she risked a fleeting glance at him. He too was trying not to laugh. After all, it was her brother who had suffered from her attempt to lighten the mood. She was incapable of speech and her hilarity was his undoing.

Theo remained frosty-faced for a few more moments and then he joined in. By the time they had recovered their composure, the atmosphere was relaxed.

'I beg your pardon for causing you to throw your ham at my brother, my lord. I also apologise for causing you to pour coffee everywhere, Theo.'

'Might I be permitted to enquire why you did such a thing?' Kit enquired.

'We were all behaving differently and I just wished to get your attention. I don't want the fact that I am marrying you to change anything between the three of us.'

He nodded as if agreeing but then

said something else entirely. 'As you will no longer be a Faulkner, will not be residing here, and will be my responsibility rather than your parents' — everything is going to change.'

Her brother smiled. 'I shall become Kit's brother and you will gain three sisters.'

She glared at both of them. 'You are being deliberately obtuse. I am not talking about such changes, as well you know. I am referring to how we behave towards each other. We have always been good friends, comfortable in each other's company. I don't wish that to be any different.'

'We know that, sweetheart, we were teasing you. It is what friends do, is it not?' Kit followed his remark by rapping her hard on the knuckles with his fork. He was becoming overfond of this behaviour and she intended to put a stop to it right now.

Without stopping to think of the consequences, she snatched up the nearest piece of cutlery and returned the favour. Inadvertently, she had grasped her knife by the blade and therefore struck him with the heavy handle.

His language turned the air blue. Her instinct was to flee, but she had already caused him serious harm and needed to know she had not broken his hand.

She was on her feet and tipping water onto a napkin before he had finished swearing at her. A cold compress on the bruise was the correct treatment. 'Let me see, I might have broken something.'

The look she received could have scorched through a lesser mortal but she was made of sterner stuff and would not be gainsaid when it came to taking care of a patient. Ministering to the sick and injured was one of the things that interested her. Despite her parents' disapproval, she had spent many days working alongside the local physician, as well as learning everything she could about the efficacious use of herbs and natural remedies.

She had set half a dozen broken limbs, lanced boils, administered to those with the influenza and applied sutures to countless injuries over the past five years. The physician had not been called to anyone on their estate since she had become so proficient in her healing skills.

She disregarded his fulminating stare and took his injured hand in hers.

'Let her look, Kit, you know she is as good as most physicians.' Her brother had moved around the table and was resting his hands on her patient's shoulders, preventing him from getting out of his chair.

Carefully she flexed his fingers. 'Nothing broken, thank the good Lord. It will be stiff and sore for a few days but I am sure you have had worse sparring with your cronies in London.' She folded the wet cloth into a pad and then held it in place with a second napkin. 'This will help ease the pain, my lord.'

His arm had relaxed whilst she was examining him. Although she had treated labourers, servants and so on, she had never been asked to treat a gentleman. His hand was unlike any other she had touched and reminded her of his bare feet which she had seen last night.

Hastily she released him. 'You must ask your valet to replace the pad. I shall send him some salve that will help bring out the bruise.'

'You may stop fussing, Helena, I refuse to be a patient of yours. I have only myself to blame for starting this game — I can assure you that I will not repeat it.'

'It was not fun for me, being rapped on the knuckles. I had no intention of hitting you quite so hard and I do apologise for that. I just wished to make it clear that I did not appreciate your gesture.'

There was a faint click of a door closing. Her brother had obviously left them to converse alone.

Kit was aware he had to tread very carefully if he was not to reveal that he had fallen in love with his future bride. If she had any inkling of his intention to court her gently and eventually persuade her to fall in love with him, she would break off the engagement immediately. Proximity should help with his plan. This was why he had suggested they take a long, intimate journey to the Lake District.

'I know you want things to remain the same between us, sweetheart, but however peculiar our marriage arrangement will be, to the outside world we shall be a normal husband and wife. The way I treat you must be seen to be different — it would not do for me to continue to treat you as a sibling. It would give rise to gossip.'

'I'm glad that you have brought that subject up, Kit. I have no wish to be the subject of unpleasant tittle-tattle or for your family to have to listen to it. Do you think we should pretend this is a love match? That we have only just realised we had feelings for each other and, as we are already well-acquainted, have decided to get married immediately?'

This was exactly what he had wanted to suggest but had been reluctant to do so. This would give him licence to behave differently, to put his hand on hers, to put his arm around her waist and whisper into her ear. His pulse quickened at the thought. Somehow, he kept his expression from showing how delighted he was.

'I think that makes perfect sense. It will only be necessary to keep up the charade whilst there are outsiders here. Your family understands the situation. Once we are married and on our own, we can revert to being good friends.' He watched closely to see if she looked even a little disappointed at this suggestion. She didn't.

'It might be wise to let Theo and your parents into the secret.'

'What about your mama and sisters? Did they know you came here expressly to offer for me?'

'No, they did not. We must dissemble with them too.'

Helena nodded. 'Will you ride with me when you have finished your conversation with my papa?'

'There is nothing I should like to do more, my love. Every moment away from you is a torment.' He clutched his chest and smiled fatuously.

She giggled as he'd hoped she would. When other young ladies did this it irritated him — but he loved the sound of her laughter.

'Fiddlesticks to that, sir. If you are going to play the fool then I shall ride on my own.'

He pushed back his chair and held out his hand. For a moment she looked at it and he thought she would refuse his gesture. Then her smile knocked him sideways.

'I am quite capable of getting out of my chair without your assistance, but your gallantry is appreciated. The more I think about it the more certain I am that I have made the right choice. There cannot be another gentleman who is as kind, thoughtful, intelligent . . . ' She stopped and tilted her head to one side. Her eyes narrowed slightly.

'Please, my dear, do go on. There is nothing a fellow likes more than to hear himself lauded in this way. I think you could add charming, handsome, athletic and brave to your list of superlatives.'

'In which case I shall also add proud, boastful, dictatorial, formidable and arrogant.'

'As we are being frank with each other, my lady, would you like me to list your attributes?'

'I should not as I am quite certain they will not be complimentary.'

'There you are quite wrong. You are indeed wilful, wild and unconventional but you are also intelligent, courageous, well-educated and wise.' He could not prevent himself smiling in a way that he thought might be too revealing. 'You are also without doubt the most beautiful woman I have ever seen.'

She jumped to her feet, ignoring his hand. She glided to the door and as she was leaving she turned. 'To be fair, I should have added that you are the most attractive gentleman of my acquaintance.'

A thrill of pleasure rippled through him. But then she smiled mischievously and continued. 'However, as I only know three gentlemen apart from you, I have not many to compare you with.'

He could hear her laughing as she ran down the passageway. The more time they spent together the more he loved her. It was going to be damnably difficult keeping to his word and not seducing her into his bed at the earliest opportunity.

He was somewhat disconcerted to find his future father-in-law so enthusiastic about the forthcoming nuptials of his daughter.

'My dear boy, I do not know why we

did not think of this solution for ourselves without the botheration of holding this house party. I cannot think there is another gentleman as suitable as yourself to be my daughter's husband.'

'It does not bother you that this is a business arrangement? My coffers are to be refilled and your daughter has a husband who will allow her to continue to study, paint and generally behave as she wishes. One who will not make any demands of her . . . '

'Good heavens, my dear boy, I do not expect you to adhere to this nonsense once you are wed. She is not a bad girl, just a little wild and has been thoroughly spoilt by myself and my wife since she was in leading strings. It was touch and go when she was born you know — I cannot think that another baby would have pulled through but she has always been a fighter.'

'I did not know that, my lord. She is the most robust young lady of my acquaintance. It is hard to imagine she was ever frail and delicate.' He would have to phrase this politely as he had no wish to offend the earl. 'However bizarre the arrangement between Helena and I, as far as we are both concerned it is a binding contract. I shall not break the terms and I am certain that neither will she. However, I am hopeful that eventually we shall both decide we wish to make it a true marriage.'

'How you conduct yourself is your own affair, my boy, but I am relieved to hear you say that one day my sweet daughter might have children of her own. Now — to business.'

Andover Hall

Richard hurled the ledger he had been studying across the room. It disintegrated when it hit the wall with a satisfying thump. He had no head for figures, could not make head nor tail of the things he had been given to look at.

God's teeth! Did he not pay his land agent, secretary and lawyers enough blunt for them to deal with all this without him having to show an interest himself?

There was a tentative knock on the study door. He roared a command to enter.

'I beg your pardon, your grace, but this letter has come by express.' The terrified footman held out a silver salver but it was shaking so much Richard found it difficult to remove it.

He gestured angrily that the man go away and he left with obvious relief. Richard had led a rackety life on his own estate and in the London house in Grosvenor Square, and was used to dealing with miserable staff, none of which understood his frustration at being cooped up here when he could be out enjoying himself.

He broke the wax seal and read the contents of the letter. He screwed it up and it followed the ledger to the far side of the room. Dammit to hell! The men he was employing to remove the obstacle to his inheritance had yet to locate the family. It had been four weeks since they had set out and he had expected them to have at least located their target by now.

He slumped back behind the desk and drained a third glass of brandy. The decanter was empty. This too was hurled at the wall and the glass shattered. He had buried his father two months ago. He could not resume his life for at least another four months. He came to a decision. He would invite his friends and their ladybirds here — if they arrived quietly, in closed carriages, no one apart from the staff would be aware he was entertaining. If his servants valued their position, they would keep their damn mouths shut.

6

Faulkner Court

'I have no wish to be married at St Andrew's, Papa, I wish to be married in our own chapel, therefore the banns should be read there and not in the village.' Helena looked at her future husband for support.

'It is the bride's prerogative to make decisions of this sort. The only disadvantage of marrying in your family chapel is the size. It will seat only twenty and there will be three times that number wishing to attend.'

'I do not see why it could not be restricted to immediate family. That would mean your mother and sisters, my brother and my parents. I have no wish for flower girls or any of that flummery. Theo can stand up for you so there is no necessity for anyone else to be present at the actual ceremony.'

Her mother smiled indulgently. 'If that is what you want, my love, then that is how it will be. James, my dear, think how much simpler it will be to have it here. We shall hold a splendid wedding breakfast for our house guests and then we shall have a ball to celebrate with our neighbours that night. Surely that is sufficient to make the day memorable?'

Papa acquiesced as he always did, eventually. 'Then so be it. The curate can read the banns tomorrow. I have placed an announcement in The Times of your forthcoming wedding, Helena. That way no one who comes to the house party will do so in false expectation.'

'Oh dear, James, do you think that was wise? Half our guests could cry off as they were well aware why they had been invited.'

'The gentlemen concerned will understand that even if the first prize is already won, there will be several other suitable young ladies on offer.'

This was the outside of enough and she could not remain silent after such an outrageous statement. She surged to her feet, her eyes flashing with indignation. 'I thought better of you, Papa. How could you refer to me as a prize and the other debutantes as being on offer? Excuse me, I am going to my studio.'

Instead of going upstairs she slipped out through a side door and headed for the rose garden. This was a favourite haunt of hers as it had several hidden arbours, honeysuckle-covered seats, and even a small summer house. It had been built for her grandmother before her time and Mama never used it as she disliked being outside.

Her anger trickled away as she walked. The sound of the skylarks, blackbirds and thrushes was enough to calm her. She strolled through the roses, pausing to admire a favourite bloom or smell the perfume of another. Roses were her favourite flowers and were to be used to decorate the chapel and the house for her wedding.

The more she considered the matter, the less sure she was that she had made a sensible decision. The advantage of marrying Kit was that she knew him so well, trusted him, liked him, loved him like a brother. The disadvantage was that he was the least compliant gentleman she had ever met. Even her brother seemed tame by comparison.

Why had he agreed to marry her? There were a dozen or more eligible heiresses he could have chosen who would make him a far better wife than she. Had he agreed to this arrangement for the same reasons she had? Next time they were together she would bring the subject up. One thing she knew for certain was he would never lie to her.

She returned to the drawing room and apologised prettily for her rudeness and, as always, her bad behaviour was immediately forgiven and forgotten.

For the next two weeks Helena hid in her tower, only coming out to change for dinner. The house was in turmoil, every surface was being cleaned and polished, every curtain shaken and every piece of cutlery, silver and crockery polished.

Kit and Theo had also made themselves scarce. Kit had returned to his own house — soon to be hers as well — to inform his mother and sisters of his forthcoming marriage. He was also making arrangements for their mythical trip to Bath, as well as their genuine trip to the Lake District. Her brother had either returned to his own estate or gone to town on business matters.

The morning that the guests were due to arrive, her mother appeared before noon. 'Helena, you must give me your word that you will not retreat to your tower during the house party. You must spend every minute with your future husband and convince our guests that this is a genuine love match.'

'I promise I will be the epitome of a loving bride-to-be, and you and Papa will have nothing with which to concern yourselves. I cannot tell you how happy I am that the house is now ready. I cannot recall an occasion when there was so much botheration.'

'All I can say, my love, is that I am relieved the Dowager Lady Drake will be running the house and not yourself.'

'Even if I wished to take over that position, I would not do so, as I have no wish to upset my future mother-in-law. Kit and I have a separate wing, we will have our own staff and I suppose I shall have no alternative but to be the lady of the house for the two of us.'

'There are things that I need to tell you about the duties of a wife . . .'

'Allow me to stop you there, Mama. I know exactly to what you are referring and know more than enough about those duties. Anyway, as you well know ours is to be a marriage of convenience and we shall not consummate the union.'

'Then I shall say no more. If you need to talk about matters of intimacy you shall be able to discuss it with Lady Drake.' From both her expression and her tone, Helena was sure her mother was only too happy to pass on this burdensome task. 'I had a message about your wardrobe. It should be here today. You will be able to wear one of your new evening gowns this evening.'

'I can see three carriages coming up the drive, Mama. I shall find Papa as he said last night that he intended to be here to greet them.'

Although she disliked being in company, Helena behaved impeccably and remained to speak personally to all the families that arrived. Mama had decided the young gentlemen should be in the east wing. The daughters of the families remained with their parents. Kit's mother and sisters were in the last empty apartment on the family side of the house.

She was relieved when the final guests arrived later that afternoon and she could retreat to her private sitting room to read in peace. Faulkner Court was of recent construction as it had been built by her grandfather. The old building had been demolished and the area turned into the rose garden.

To her it seemed an unnecessary extravagance to erect such a large building when it would only have to house half a dozen adults and a handful of children. Of course, the servants had to have accommodation, but even so she could see no necessity for a dozen bedchambers for family members and a further dozen for visitors. This was the first time in her lifetime all the rooms would be occupied. Heaven knows where the extra staff were to sleep, but that was not her concern.

She was curled up in the window seat, staring pensively out of the window, when there was a knock on her sitting room door. Mary, who had been in the dressing room unpacking her new garments, hurried through and opened the door.

'Kit, when did you arrive? I had thought you were going to travel with your family who arrived several hours ago.'

He strolled across and folded his long, lean length onto a nearby chair. He was not his usual charming self; he seemed troubled and this bothered her. She swung her legs to the floor. 'What's wrong, Kit? Have you changed your mind about tomorrow?'

His face cleared and his smile warmed her. 'I am a man of my word, sweetheart. No, something odd is happening and I think it is probably best to tell you the whole.' He stopped and seemed lost in thought again.

She prodded him with her outstretched hand. 'Well, tell me then. Do not keep me in suspense.'

'One of my tenants, a reliable man, told me in confidence that there were strangers in the neighbourhood making enquiries about me and my family. I

110

have no notion what this might be about and could find no trace of these men myself.' He frowned and ran his fingers through his hair, a familiar gesture that she found endearing. 'I have left my agent to continue making enquiries.'

'Have you borrowed money and not repaid it?' His expression changed and for a second he looked so fierce she did not recognise him.

'I owe nothing.' Then he relaxed and was her Kit again. 'I am taking some precautions. I came to tell you of my plans.'

'I am glad you and your family are here. They will be safe at Faulkner Court for the summer, so you can go away without worrying.'

'I have spoken to the earl and he has agreed to keep them here until we return from Bath. I have also arranged for us to be accompanied by four armed outriders just to be sure.'

'That seems rather extreme.' A flicker of annoyance warned her not to continue on this track. 'It is your prerogative to do as you wish. I was not suggesting otherwise, so there is no need to look so disapproving.'

'You read me too well, sweetheart. I rather think you shall run me ragged once we are united. I have an outlandish suggestion. Would you consider leaving the morning after our wedding? I should much prefer to be travelling with you rather than being obliged to do the pretty to dozens of strangers. Also, I shall be happier away from here and travelling to the north when all think we go to Bath.'

She threw her arms around him. He stiffened and immediately she stepped away, her face scarlet. 'I beg your pardon, I must remember not to be so rag-mannered in future. I should love to leave after the ball, for whatever reason. In fact, I shall consider it your wedding gift to me for I could not have a better one.'

★　★　★

'I had not considered giving you a gift: as it is not a true marriage, I do not think you are entitled to one.'

She kicked his shin, but as she was wearing indoor slippers it hurt her more than it did him. 'How can you say such a thing? I shall be asked what you gave me at the ball and . . . '

'I was teasing you, my dear. I have the required gift. No, do not flutter your eyelashes at me, you baggage, I will not reveal it until we are wed tomorrow.'

As she resumed her place on the window seat she curled her legs under her and he got a delightful glimpse of bare ankles. She was not wearing stockings. He was on his feet and striding to the door before his embarrassment could be seen.

'You will need to get your maid to pack your trunks if we are to leave the day after tomorrow.' He was out of the room as if pursued by wolves and into his own apartment. Duncan, his valet, had accompanied him this time and was busy laying out his evening rig in the bedchamber.

He glanced through the window and saw the ornamental lake. He would take a dip in there. That would cool his ardour. God knows how he was to maintain the pretence of being a friend to his beloved when what he wanted was to make love to her.

He had used the excuse of the strangers to bring forward their departure. Not because he had no wish to socialise but because he had no intention of sharing her with anyone. He was certain she was not indifferent to him. They would sometimes be obliged to share a bedchamber on the journey which would give him ample opportunity to court her.

He had told her he was employing four armed men to make the need to leave more urgent. This meant that now he had to find some as he had no wish to be shown up as a liar. He was a little concerned about why these men were enquiring about him, but not unduly so. His agent, Forester, was more than competent to search out the answer.

The grass was springy under his boots and he was obliged to watch his footing to avoid stepping in deer and sheep dung. No doubt an army of outside servants would sweep the area clean before the garden party which was to be held for the villagers and tenants, as well as the guests.

He was surprised that Helena had not wished to remain for this as she had been excited about the thought of the entertainment that was to be provided. The lake looked less inviting when he arrived. There was a copious amount of green weed floating on the surface and he changed his mind about swimming.

The need to take a cool dip had also gone. He loosened his cravat and shrugged off his jacket. Strolling around in one's shirtsleeves would probably be frowned upon by anyone who saw him, but he cared not. He was his own man, always had been. He followed the rules when it would be wise to do so but otherwise ignored them.

His mouth curved. His future bride was cut from the same cloth. They would make a perfect match. The stables beckoned and as he waited for a groom to saddle his massive stallion, he remembered that Theo had told him something about this young man that might be of help.

'Am I right in thinking that your brother is looking for employment? Was he not in the militia until recently?'

'That's right, my lord. Bill got a bullet in his leg and can't march any more. He ain't the only one fit enough to work but not to serve King and Country.'

'I need four men to accompany my wife and I on our wedding trip. They will be outriders, but also act as grooms and in any other capacity I deem necessary.'

'My pa's the blacksmith in the village. You'll find my Bill helping out there. He'll find you the other three what you need, sir.'

Kit tossed the man a coin, mounted his horse, and headed for the village. He knew exactly where the blacksmith's forge was situated as he had had occasion to visit on more than one occasion over the past years. There was a farmhorse being shod. The young man holding his head nodded to him.

'Are you Bill, by any chance? Your brother sent me to speak to you. I am Lord Drake and am seeking men to act as outriders on my wedding trip.'

The smith looked up from hammering a shoe. 'Tie Betsy to the post, son, she'll not shift. You go along with his lordship.'

The young man's limp was not as bad as he had feared. They stepped out into the cooler air outside the smithy before talking.

'I'm seeking employment, my lord. I'm handy with my fists, can fire a musket or a pistol, and an expert around horses.'

'Then I shall be happy to take you on. I shall be even happier if you can find me three others with similar skills. I shall expect you to be vigilant whilst we are travelling, act as grooms, and ride ahead to book accommodation when necessary.'

'I can do that, sir. I can also find you the other men. Do they have to have been soldiers?'

'Not necessarily — as long as they can handle a weapon, that will be sufficient.'

The young man, half a head shorter than himself but almost as broad, touched his cap and beamed. 'I've a younger brother, he's been working as a gamekeeper's assistant but ain't too happy there. I reckon I'll have no trouble finding the other two. There ain't much permanent work around here and a few months travelling the country is a sight better than slaving in a field.'

Kit hid his smile. If this young man was as efficient at his work as he was with his tongue then he would be satisfied. 'I shall leave the matter to you then, Bill. Report to Faulkner Court in two days' time. I shall supply your weapons and mounts.'

The matter settled satisfactorily for both parties, he rode back, confident he would not now be revealed as being untruthful. The earl had already transferred an enormous sum to his coffers — if he had not, then the employment of four extra men, plus horseflesh for them, would not have been possible.

* * *

Helena barely had time to speak to Kit before her wedding day. They had stolen a few minutes together on the terrace when he had told her everything was in place for their departure. The sun shone, the house was sparkling and even the grounds were looking immaculate. She was sorry to be missing the entertainment, but she would much rather be travelling to the Lake District with Kit.

Mama came in to inspect her

ensemble before she went down to the chapel. 'My darling girl, you look everything I ever dreamt you would. For a young lady who is marrying for expedience you look remarkably happy.'

'I am, Mama, I am ready for my new adventure.'

'You will be able to attend assemblies in Bath and wear all your new gowns. I think duck-egg blue with the turquoise sash and beading is absolutely perfect with your russet hair. Are you quite sure you do not wish to carry a bouquet of any sort?'

'I do not. Shall we go down? I do not wish to keep my groom waiting.'

Papa threaded her arm through his and patted her hand. 'I cannot believe my baby girl is now old enough to marry. Drake is a lucky man. Are you quite sure you wish to go through with this?'

'I think it is rather late to be changing my mind. I am confident that I am making the right decision.'

The guests had gathered in the vast

entrance hall and she walked through them, basking in their approval. It was not often she was approved of by anyone apart from her family.

Kit was talking to Theo when she entered the chapel but somehow he sensed she was there and turned. The smile he sent her almost convinced her he was actually pleased to be marrying her because he loved her. He really was the most consummate play-actor.

Her response was equally radiant and instead of waiting, he walked towards her. 'You look quite *ravissante*, my love, that gown is a triumph.' He threaded her hand through his arm and they walked together the remaining distance.

The curate beamed. They both made their responses in loud, clear voices so those waiting in the corridor outside the chapel would be able to hear, even if they could not see the proceedings. There were to be no prayers, homilies or hymns, which was a relief as she was not overfond of any of them.

In no time at all she was transformed

from Lady Helena Faulkner to Lady Helena Drake. A small difference in name but a vast one in her circumstances. Before she could protest, he tilted her face and placed a tender kiss on her parted lips. This was not part of the bargain but his expression was amused and she refused to rise to his provoking.

'It is hard to credit, Kit, that we have changed our lives so radically in so short a space of time.'

'A change for the better, sweetheart, as you will discover. I cannot wait to begin our journey to Bath.'

'I intend to take the waters, visit the sights and attend all the assemblies and concerts. What are you going to do, my lord?'

His shout of laughter echoed around the chapel. 'You are incorrigible. Come, I am sharp-set and I believe there is a sumptuous wedding breakfast awaiting us in the dining room. Champagne is to be served and I suggest that you imbibe no more than a mouthful or two.

Alcohol goes to your head, if I remember rightly.'

'You promised never to mention that embarrassing incident again. I did not intend to drive your curricle into the duck pond. Anyway, you are so much older than me and should have had more sense than to allow me to take the ribbons when I was a trifle bosky.'

'You certainly were. So, we are in agreement on the subject? You will stick to coffee or lemonade and have only a mouthful for the toast.'

A ripple of unease ran through her. They had only been married five minutes and already he was telling her how to behave. This was not part of the agreement. The fact that he was right made no difference.

'As the toast will be to ourselves there is no necessity for me to drink any at all.' His expression of relief was comical. 'Nevertheless, my love, I intend to consume whatever I wish at our celebration ball tonight.'

There was no time for him to

reprimand her as they had reached the dining room. Usually people seated themselves as they arrived but today things were more formal. The bridal pair, she noticed, were to sit at the head of the table. They were to be flanked on one side by her parents and brother and on the other by his mother and sisters. After that the guests sat as they wished.

It might be called breakfast and be the first meal of the day but it bore more resemblance to a grand dinner. The toast was made first, an error in her eyes as this meant champagne was circulating before the food was on the table. As the meal progressed, so the noise got louder. Even her mama was flushed and talkative.

It would appear that only Kit and herself had remained abstemious. She touched him on his elbow. 'I am not comfortable here. Would it be considered appalling behaviour on my part if I were to leave?'

'Not if I come with you. They will

just assume we are retiring to celebrate our union.'

She placed her napkin on her plate of untouched food and waited for him to pull her chair back. He put his arm around her waist to escort her out and every eye in the room was scorching her back. Her cheeks were scarlet. She had never been so embarrassed in her life as she was by the nudges, winks, and knowing smiles she had received on her way out.

'You ate nothing. Wait for me in your sitting room and I shall bring you something. Then perhaps you would like to ride out with me?'

He didn't stay for her response, just assumed she would do as he said. She was not a child to disobey his every word just because she did not like to be dictated to. If what he said was what she actually wanted to do then she would do it — otherwise she would ignore his commands.

Mary helped her into her habit. 'I should like a bath drawn at six o'clock.

I do not want to put on my new ballgown smelling of the stable. I shall not require your assistance until then so you may have the remainder of the afternoon to yourself.'

The trunks were already loaded onto the carriage in which her abigail and his valet were to travel. It was to leave at dawn and she and Kit would follow soon afterwards. The coachman, who was loyal to a fault, knew they were not going to Bath, but their servants did not. She smiled at the thought of their confusion when they discovered they were in fact on their way to the Lake District.

When she emerged from her dressing room and entered her sitting room, it was to find her husband there before her. On the table in front of the window was a delicious array of items. Her stomach gurgled loudly and he chuckled.

'I am glad this repast meets with your approval, sweetheart. I shall join you. I too did not do the breakfast justice.'

126

7

The horses Kit had acquired for the four outriders were sturdy animals and ideal for their purpose. His stallion and her gelding would be led initially; he thought it better to depart in the carriage, as sensible people would do.

He called the head groom over. 'I require suitable mounts saddled for myself and Lady Helena. I do not want to overtax the horses we are taking with us.'

'Her ladyship can ride anything in the stable and we have two that are up to your weight, my lord.'

'Then I shall leave the choice to you. We wish to go out immediately.'

He wandered through the archway towards the side door through which his new bride would leave the house. A month ago he had been in low spirits, at a loss to know how he would be able to maintain his estate without starting to sell off farms and land. He had decided he had no option but to marry an heiress but had never dreamt it would be Helena.

He leaned against the wall, out of the bright sunshine and all was right in his world. He had married the girl he had been in love with for years — although he had not realised it until a few weeks ago — and was sanguine that eventually he would have the perfect union.

The door opened and he stepped forward. 'I do not believe there is another young lady in the county who can change her raiment so speedily. Our horses are waiting, sweetheart, and so am I.'

There was little opportunity for conversation during the hectic two hours they spent charging over the countryside, jumping ditches and hedges and generally enjoying themselves. Her face was streaked with mud, her glorious russet hair tumbling around her shoulders and her military-style cap long gone.

She had never looked more beautiful.

He didn't offer to help her dismount, she was quite capable of doing this herself. She turned to him with a smile that made him want to pull her into his arms and show her just how much he loved her.

'That was most enjoyable. We are to dine at seven. Will you escort me?'

'I shall come to your apartment as I have yet to give you your gift.'

He rubbed the dirt from her cheek with his thumb and she stood on tiptoes to do the same for him. 'I rather think I'm going to enjoy being married to you, Kit. I cannot think why we did not do it before this.'

'Neither can I, sweetheart, I believe we are ideally matched. I fear this evening is going to be a riotous occasion if the noise from the house is anything to go by. The young gentlemen are already drunk as wheelbarrows — let us hope they sober up a little before they start drinking again at dinner.'

'We can retire early and leave them to it. I suppose we must open the ball, then dance with family members before we escape.'

'I sincerely hope our mamas do not intend to get up to wave us away.'

'At that time of the morning? I should think not — my mother is rarely seen before noon.'

They used the secondary stairs again and she vanished with a flick of her skirt into her apartment. He had no intention of going downstairs before he had to, so decided he would check his notes to ensure his plans for their extended trip had no flaws.

His lips curved as he imagined her reaction when she discovered that as a couple on their honeymoon they would be expected to share a bed most nights. His intention was to sleep on the floor. His self-control was legendary but being in the same bed as the woman he desired would be more than even he could deal with.

The gift he had for her was a parure

that apparently had belonged to his father's grandmother. The tiara, the necklace and ear-bobs were of emeralds and diamonds set in gold. Duncan had enquired from her maid and so he knew her ballgown was emerald green silk. These jewels would be perfect.

His father had never discussed his family. When he had questioned his mama about them, she had said she thought his grandfather might have been a duke but she was not certain. It appeared his father's choice of bride had not pleased this illustrious aristocrat and they had never spoken again. Papa must have been the youngest son as he could not have abandoned his family so easily otherwise.

He might have cousins, uncles and aunts that he knew nothing about. Maybe when they got back from their travels he would start to make enquiries. The only thing he knew for certain was that Audley Manor was not linked to the Drake family. His parents had moved there shortly after their marriage. Mama had told him she had no family, she had been brought up by her grandparents who were now dead.

It was hard to imagine that his quiet, studious papa was the black sheep of his family. Mind you, giving up the life he had led to marry the woman he loved also seemed out of character. He wished he had known his parent better, but too late to repine. If he was ever blessed with sons he would make sure he did a better job.

He was immersed in his papers when there was a sharp knock on the door. Before he could respond, it swung open and Theo marched in.

'Good, I hoped I would find you alone. There is something you need to know. Burgess, the estate manager, reported to my father that someone has been making enquiries about you. Have you any idea what this is about?'

'Tarnation take it! I heard the same just before I left home. They have followed me here. It is a mystery to me why anyone would wish to do this rather than approach me directly.'

'No outraged husbands? Jilted lovers?'

Kit's stomach clenched. 'I did not inform my mistress of my wedding plans. Elizabeth is a passionate and jealous woman but she has always known I would never marry her. It is possible she has sent her servants to see if I actually married Helena today.' He thought about this for a moment and then shook his head. 'No, it cannot be her. She would have no need to send men to ask questions as she is well aware of who I am and where I live.'

'That may be the case, my friend. She might well have seen the announcement in The Times, so your mistress would have been aware you were to be married. If you did not inform her yourself, she might well be angry and intend to cause you embarrassment.'

'Devil take it! I have done exactly that and Elizabeth would not take kindly to my disrespect. However, I am no longer concerned about these men as they have now got the information they required and will have returned to London with it. I can assure you that your sister is in no danger from that direction. My mistress, or should I say my previous mistress, will accept the marriage as a *fait accompli* and look elsewhere.'

Theo was not impressed. 'A gentleman would have severed the connection before marrying. This is not well done of you, Kit.'

'I should have done so but I have been somewhat occupied these past two weeks with getting my house ready for your sister. Did you know that my family is remaining here for the summer to allow the builders and carpenters to work unfettered by their occupation?'

'I did not, but the place will seem sadly empty with Helena gone and having your mama and sisters in residence will be good for my parents.'

The gong sounded loudly in the hall

indicating that it was time for the guests to return to their chambers and change for dinner. As there was to be a ball following the meal, preparations, especially for the ladies, would be more elaborate and take far longer than was usual.

'I doubt I shall have time to say a formal farewell to you as we are leaving at dawn tomorrow.'

'When do you expect to return? Bath, if I recollect correctly, is full of elderly people taking the waters.'

Kit laughed. 'True, but there are also weekly assemblies, interesting historical and picturesque places to visit, so we shall not be unoccupied. We might well travel elsewhere so do not expect us to return until the autumn.'

* * *

Helena rotated slowly in front of the full-length glass, admiring her appearance. Emerald green silk was not an accepted colour for unmarried ladies but perfectly respectable now. The jewellery Kit had given her complemented her ensemble.

'My lady, I have never seen you look so well. The colour exactly matches your eyes,' her maid said as she stood back to inspect her handiwork.

'I shall not need you tonight, Mary, so make sure you retire early as you must be away from here at first light. I am sad that I cannot take this beautiful gown, but I have two others almost as handsome and they will have to suffice.'

Kit strolled in without knocking — she supposed as her husband he was entitled to do so now. She caught her breath. He had never looked more attractive than he did tonight. Evening dress was perfect on his tall frame but, as she had seen him in it several times before, why had she only just noticed this fact?

'Your waistcoat is made of the same silk as my gown. How did you achieve that miracle?'

He bowed with a flourish. 'I am a

resourceful gentleman, my love, and seeing us dressed as we are will serve our cause and convince our guests that this is indeed a love match. Do you think you can simper and hang on my every word this evening?'

'I shall do my best, my lord, after all, am I not the most submissive and obedient of wives?'

He held out his arm and she slipped hers through it. There was no need for dissembling; she did love him, but not in the way a wife should love her husband. She loved him like a brother. Tonight, though, she would play the part of a happy bride as she had no wish to cause her parents or his mama any embarrassment.

When they reached the head of the stairs he paused. 'Allow me to say, sweetheart, that you will be the most beautiful young lady at this ball. This might be an unusual arrangement, but I am certain we shall be happy together.'

'You will certainly be one of the most attractive gentlemen attending, Kit.

137

However, I believe that Theo will outshine you.'

The dinner was less elaborate than usual as there would be a substantial supper served at eleven o'clock. Helena scarcely knew what she ate; she picked at her food, finding it difficult to swallow. Being the centre of attention was something she abhorred and she was relieved when her mother finally rose from her seat to lead the ladies from the room.

The lanterns and flambeaux danced in the breeze, adding enchantment to the evening. The first carriages would be here at any moment and, as the bride and groom, she and Kit must stand at the head of the line to greet everyone.

She was tempted to slip away, standing nodding and smiling for an hour or more did not appeal to her. Then her husband was behind her and prevented her escape. 'It will be tedious, my love, but we have no option. It is expected of us.'

With his arm firmly around her waist, he guided her across the vast hall and positioned them next to her parents. Lady Drake was next, but there was no sign of her brother, or his sisters. This was a good thing as it meant the guests would move more quickly into the ballroom and she and Kit would be free to mingle.

He made the experience as enjoyable as it could be with whispered comments about the guests that made her laugh. Eventually the last arrivals had been greeted.

'The musicians are tuning up, you and Kit must hurry, Helena, as you will be leading the first set.'

Her husband nodded politely to his mother-in-law but winked at her. They were halfway down the passageway when she realised they were not playing the opening bars of a country dance but of a waltz — the new, daring dance that had recently arrived from the continent.

'Kit, Mama will be scandalised and I might embarrass us both. I've never performed this dance in public.'

'Neither have I, my love, but I am confident I can lead you safely around the floor.'

As soon as they entered, a ripple of anticipation ran around the assembled spectators. She almost missed her step but he held her steady.

'Kit, we shall be the only ones dancing. No one else looks ready to join us on the floor.'

'I sincerely hope so, sweetheart, as that is what I planned.'

There was no time for her to protest as he twirled her away. After the first few steps she relaxed and began to enjoy the experience. He was no novice but an expert and all she had to do was follow his lead. As the final notes died away, he bowed and she curtsied and the ballroom erupted into applause.

'That was quite wonderful, thank you, Kit. Do we have to dance with other guests or can we escape immediately?'

'It would be extremely impolite to

leave before supper. They are now having the country dance and we shall lead the first set. Your guests have come to celebrate our nuptials, you have no option but to enjoy yourself.'

Indeed, the evening passed so quickly she scarcely had time to remember that she didn't enjoy social events. Just before supper, champagne was served and several toasts were made in their honour.

'Now we can retire, sweetheart, no one will think it odd of us to wish to be alone on our wedding night.' He said this with a commendably straight face but his smile was wicked.

Something prompted her to respond to his teasing. She stepped in closer, stood on tiptoes and in full view of the company, kissed him on the lips. There was a collective gasp from around her and she immediately regretted her impulsive action.

Then, to her shock, his arms pulled her tight so every inch of her was crushed against him. Then his mouth closed over hers and she was swept away to a place she hadn't known existed. Her legs would have crumpled beneath her if he had not been holding her upright.

He raised his head and his smile made her head spin. Then he took her hand and they ran from the shocked circle of guests who had witnessed their disgraceful behaviour. Once they were safely out of sight, they slowed their pace.

'That will give the tabbies something to talk about, sweetheart, it was exactly the right thing for you to do. There will not be a person in this house who doesn't believe we have married for love. Your secret will be safe.'

He released her hand and for some reason she felt bereft, wanting him to take it again. They arrived at her sitting room. 'Good night, Helena. I cannot wait to show you the beauties of our country.'

'And I cannot wait to see them. I must own that I have not once thought about my work in the tower. I rather think that being married to you could well be more exciting than studying molluscs and painting watercolours of my discoveries.'

His laughter warmed her as she hurried into her apartment for what was to be the last time. Something they had not discussed was the fact that if they were to keep their unusual marital arrangements secret from the staff, they would be obliged to make other plans. Mama and Papa did not share a room but had their own bedchambers. This would suit her very well and she was certain Kit would not object either.

The beautiful gown was draped carefully over the stand put out to receive it. She added the matching gloves and evening slippers. Her habit was waiting for her, as were the necessary underpinnings, her riding boots, hat and gloves. Her maid and the luggage would be leaving an hour or two before them and would come in and rouse her before she left.

It seemed as if she scarcely had her head on the pillow for a quarter of an hour before she was awoken.

'There is no need for you to help me dress, Mary. Lord Drake and I will see you this evening when we overnight.'

There was hot water in the jug and she quickly completed her ablutions and was dressed in minutes. The bedchambers were quiet, none of the guests would appear until midday at the earliest. Servants would be busy restoring the ballroom to its former pristine state. She was sad to be missing the garden party, but it was being held mainly for the villagers and staff and they would not mind if she and Kit were absent.

She checked the overmantel clock — they were not to leave until thirty minutes past five — she was too impatient to wait up here for half an hour so would go down to the stables and tack up her own horse.

★ ★ ★

Kit was in the yard to ensure that the carriage with his valet and Helena's maid left promptly. Duncan was more his man of affairs than his personal servant and would be making the arrangements for their journey as they went. His first task would be to have a breakfast waiting for them when they arrived at the Goat and Boot, a hostelry two hours' ride from here.

The carriage would then continue on its way, allowing him to make a leisurely journey with his bride to the inn at which they were going to spend their first night. Two of his recently employed outriders were accompanying the carriage so one or other could ride ahead or seek him out if there were any messages. The other two would follow behind him. If there was a mishap of any sort, if a horse lost a shoe or fell lame, or either of them took a tumble, it would be useful having these men close by.

He glanced at his gold pocket watch. Helena would be down in half an hour if she did not oversleep. However, she appeared in the stable yard a few minutes later looking as eager as he to get started. 'Good morning, sweetheart, I did not expect you so soon.'

'I was too excited to remain in my apartment. Are you ready to depart now or do we have to wait until the designated time?'

He snapped his fingers and their horses were led out. 'As you may observe, I too wish to get started on this adventure.'

She gathered her reins and turned for him to grasp her boot and toss her into the saddle. He didn't offer to put her foot into the stirrup iron, she was quite capable of doing that for herself. He mounted his stallion and twisted in the saddle to check the men were also ready.

'We have no need to rush, there's only a few miles to cover before we stop to break our fast.'

'You neglected to show me our itinerary, Kit, perhaps you could do so when we halt?'

'I have only the one copy and Duncan has it. It will be his task to keep us to our route and arrange for our accommodation and refreshments.'

'I wonder how long it will take for our family to realise we have not gone to Bath,' she said.

'Unless they are expecting a regular supply of letters from you, I see no reason why they should be aware that we have gone elsewhere.'

'Knowing Mama, she might well make enquiries from a bosom bow of hers who lives permanently in that city. She will know that we are not in residence within a sennight. Papa will set up a hue and cry, convinced we have met a grisly end somewhere on the road.'

'In which case, sweetheart, you must write to them tomorrow and send the letter by express. I have no wish for them to be unduly concerned for your welfare.'

'I wish now that we had told them what we planned. I cannot see that you would have been gainsaid on this matter.'

'No, but I had no wish to upset them. Better they are not aware of our unconventional plans until it is too late for them to make objections.'

8

Andover Hall

Richard snatched the letter from the silver salver being held out to him by his butler and broke the seal. He read the contents and his face twisted into a snarl. He screwed up the paper and threw it across the room.

How could the imbeciles have lost the couple they had been sent to assassinate? All they had to do was wait in a suitably deserted place and hold up the carriage as if they were highwaymen. Yet now it appeared his quarry had vanished into thin air.

He had been uncomfortable about adding Drake's new bride to their list, but he couldn't risk the wretched girl producing a male heir next year. They both had to die in order to secure his title. He could not risk employing further men on this grisly task so would have to rely on those he had already working for him.

The letter had said they were retracing their steps and were confident they would eventually find them. He wanted this done before the six months were up so there would be another three months to complete the job.

Those he had invited to stay to alleviate the boredom had been sent packing. For some reason he had not enjoyed their company, had not wanted to drink and gamble to excess and enjoy the favours of the light-skirts that had accompanied his cronies.

He slumped into the chair behind the desk. If being a duke meant he must moulder in this barracks of a place surrounded by cowed servants then he would renounce his title but keep the money.

* * *

'This is a delightful hostelry, Kit, I shall be comfortable here and our horses will be well taken care of in their stables.' Helena dropped to the cobbles and patted the animal's neck. 'I have never enjoyed a day so much, we have viewed picturesque ruins, paddled in a river and eaten a delicious picnic in a wood.'

'Our mounts will be ready to leave first thing. I shall just speak to my coachman and then join you inside.'

He strode away, every inch an aristocrat, and not for the first time that day she thanked the Lord for allowing her to marry him. Mary was waiting in the foyer to conduct her to her chambers.

'This way, my lady, everything is ready for you upstairs.'

The building was of relatively modern construction and the ceilings were high; no danger of her husband cracking his head on a beam. She followed her maid into a pretty, well-appointed sitting room.

'His lordship's bedchamber is adjacent to yours and there's a communicating door.'

'Excellent. Do you have somewhere pleasant to sleep?'

'I do, my lady, the female staff have rooms together in the attic and the male are on the right. Unfortunately, there's no bell there to tell me if you require my services.'

'I shall not need you until seven o'clock tomorrow morning. If you go down and fetch my hot water and bring it to me then that will be satisfactory.'

Her night things had been carefully put out on the bottom of the bed and there was ample hot water to complete a strip wash. Freshly attired in a blue sprigged muslin gown, she walked into the sitting room to find Kit ready before her.

'At last, I thought we could take a stroll around the gardens before we eat. That's a pretty gown, sweetheart, blue suits you perfectly even though you have green eyes.'

She moved closer and stared up at him. 'If you had asked me yesterday what colour your eyes were I would have been unable to tell you. Now I see they are a dark blue, almost black; a perfect match to your dark colouring.'

'My father informed me that all males in the Drake family have these peculiar eyes. You must not forget to write your letter after we have eaten. I have already arranged for it to be delivered.'

In this short missive she explained to her parents that they had changed their mind at the last minute and decided to travel to the Lake District instead of spending several weeks in Bath. She told them she was happy, but they were not to worry as her husband was perfectly capable of taking care of her in every circumstance. Satisfied with what she'd written, she sanded the paper, carefully folded it into a square and sealed it with a blob of wax.

'Here, you must use this,' he said from right behind her. For a big man he moved as stealthily as a panther.

'Thank you, is that the family seal?'

'It is. I believe it to be the only thing

153

my father had from his past life.'

'May I examine it before you put it back?'

He dropped it into her palm, still warm from his finger. She held the crest up to the light. She blinked and looked again, unsure if what she'd seen was imagination or actually there. After taking it to the window to examine it more closely, she was convinced.

'Did you know you have a ducal crest on it? Are you nobility, not just aristocracy?'

He shrugged. 'Papa never spoke about his past, but my mother mentioned once that she thought my grandfather might be a duke. I have never looked into it, but I will do so if you are curious.'

'Not particularly. It makes no matter to me who your ancestors were. I did not marry them, I married you.'

His smile made her toes curl in her slippers and she had no idea why this strange phenomenon had taken place. 'Your pedigree is impeccable too. We are indeed an excellent match in all respects.'

She wasn't sure if he was serious or teasing so decided to ignore this remark. 'Here, if this letter is to go by express, had you not better take it downstairs?' Issuing so abrupt an order was a mistake. His expression changed from friendly to formidable in an instant.

He held out his hand but she was wary of approaching him when he was in this mood. 'I do apologise for my abrupt command. I shall rephrase it. My lord, would you be so kind as to take this letter downstairs for me so that it might be delivered to my parents as speedily as possible?' She smiled, but it was a poor effort.

In two strides he was next to her. 'Sweetheart, you must not look so fearful. I am an irascible fellow but I would never harm you.'

Her hands were clammy, her head was spinning and she was unable to respond. She raised her hand to indicate she understood and inadvertently placed it on his chest. His heart was hammering beneath her touch and she withdrew her fingers as if touching something hot.

She wasn't sure what was happening between them. Why in that moment had things changed? Then the feeling had gone and he pinched her cheek rather harder than was necessary. 'Run along, sweetheart, you need to retire now as we will be up early.'

'Good night, Kit, thank you for a wonderful day.'

How her legs carried her into the bedchamber she did not know. She collapsed as soon as the doors closed into an undignified heap on the floor. It took her some time to recover her composure and find the energy to push herself upright.

She undressed quickly and pulled on her nightgown. The room was flooded with sunlight; she would never sleep if she could not block it out somehow. There were no curtains on the windows or around the bed to draw so she was at a loss to know what she could do.

On closer examination she discovered there were shutters on the outside that could be pulled together. These were used to keep out the inclement weather, not sunlight, but she thought if she could somehow find a way to close them they would serve the purpose.

The first window proved no problem as she was able to lean out and grab the wood and pull them closed. However, those at the other window proved recalcitrant. Kit must be back from his errand as she could hear him moving about in his bedchamber.

Forgetting she was in her nightwear, she went to the communicating door and knocked loudly. 'Kit, I need your assistance. Could I ask you to come in for a moment?'

There was no answer immediately but then there was movement and the door swung open. He had bare feet, and his topcoat, neckcloth and waist-coat had been removed, leaving him in shirt and breeches. The strong column of his neck was visible. For some reason, she could not take her eyes from it.

As she watched, his eyes darkened and a flush of colour ran along his cheekbones. Her breath caught in her throat as wave after wave of heat travelled from her toes to her crown. What was happening to her? Did she have the ague?

Her feet moved of their own volition until every inch of her was touching him. For a second he remained rigid then with what sounded like a groan, his arms were around her pulling her even closer. She tilted her head to allow him access to her mouth and he needed no further encouragement.

★   ★   ★

Kit forced his desire down, lifted her from her feet and gently placed her inside her own chamber and firmly shut the door. He rested his forehead against it, horrified by what he'd almost done. She was not much younger than him in years but a complete innocent when it came to matters of the heart. In future he must treat her as he had always done, like a younger sister, not the woman he was in love with and wanted to tumble into his bed at the first opportunity.

He walked across to the washstand and filled the china basin with cold water then plunged his head in. He remained immersed for a minute and then snatched up a towel and dried his hair as best he could. More or less restored, he returned to the door and knocked on it. On receiving no answer, he pushed it open and walked in.

She was sitting on the bed disconsolately with her head resting on her knees. 'You want me to do something for you, Helena? Was it the shutters?' This time she responded with a brief nod. Somehow, she had managed to close one pair but the other remained open. He dragged them shut and dropped the catch across to hold them in place. The room was now dark enough for her to sleep.

'Kit, I don't understand what is happening to me. I am behaving quite out of character, as are you.'

He turned and made his way to the bed but was careful to take his place as far away from her as was possible. 'Your mother should have explained this to you. We are both young, attractive, healthy individuals and spending time together alone has brought our natural inclinations to the surface. I am a man and cannot help but respond to your beauty when you are in my arms.'

'That is all very well, but it does not explain why I allowed you to kiss me. I might be an innocent, but I'm well aware that intimate embraces can only lead to further unwelcome activities. I have no wish to become your true wife and it was agreed between us that I should not. In future you will not take liberties with my person. A gentleman does not break his word as you have. Do I make myself quite clear?'

How was it that one minute he wished to make love to her and in the next to put her over his knee? No one had the temerity to speak to him like this, to dismiss him as if he were of no account. He towered above her and she flinched away from him as if expecting physical retaliation.

'I apologise if I have offended you. You might be naïve, but I would have thought even you would know that appearing in my bedchamber in nothing but your nightgown was an invitation. You arc not a child — do not behave like one.'

The bed creaked and before he could react she cannoned into him, sending him sprawling to the floor. He wasn't sure if this was accidental or deliberate.

'Get out of here, you are despicable. If you had not already spent my inheritance I should have the marriage set aside.'

He rolled over and was on his feet in

an instant. His eyes had adjusted to the darkness and he moved fast, closing the distance between them, barely able to contain his rage.

Instead of cringing away, she raised her chin and glared back at him, daring him to do his worst. His fury vanished like snow in sunshine, to be replaced by something else entirely. He daren't remain beside her a moment longer or he would be unable to restrain his passion. He spoke from the doorway.

'Good night. Be downstairs ready to leave at seven o'clock.'

'Am I to have no breakfast? Also, my maid will not be here until then so I cannot possibly be ready to leave at that time. You will just have to wait until I am ready. Kindly close the door behind you.'

His mouth curved. She was an original and his marriage was going to be anything but boring.

★   ★   ★

Helena found the next two days less enjoyable than the first. Kit was unfailingly polite to her but there was a reserve in his behaviour that hadn't been there before. This was entirely her own fault. He had been quite right to point out that parading in nothing but her nightgown must have seemed like an invitation. After all, did he not keep a mistress to slake his physical needs? This woman would not be available to him for months — would he look elsewhere?

The thought of him doing so brought tears to her eyes. His previous liaisons were no business of hers but despite her saying he could continue to see this woman she would be devastated if he did. He was riding ahead with one of his men, leaving her to her own devices. This gave her the perfect opportunity to watch him closely.

The more she looked, the faster her pulse raced. It was as if there had been a barrier of some sort between her and her husband that had suddenly lifted.

Her mouth rounded in shock. She kicked her horse violently and he responded by breaking into a gallop.

Her precipitous arrival caused both horses to shy violently. Unfortunately, her husband was standing in his stirrups looking over the hedge at that precise moment. The result was inevitable. He catapulted into the air and vanished over the foliage.

The air turned blue. Thank goodness! He was unhurt if he could use such language. The branches were torn aside and he shoved his way through, regardless of the thorns and brambles.

What a sensible young lady would have done when faced with such fury was gallop away into the distance until he had recovered his temper. What she did was drop to the ground and rush towards him.

'Kit, I am so sorry for your mishap. I have just discovered the most remarkable fact . . . ' Her words froze in her throat. He did not look in the mood to hear such a revelation.

'Good God, madam, have you taken leave of your senses? What the devil were you thinking?'

She steadied her breathing. 'I was thinking that I love you and wish to be your true wife.'

He rocked back on his heels and for a dreadful moment she thought her news might be unwelcome. Then his roar of delight caused her mount to bolt and the unfortunate outrider now had two horses to fetch back.

He picked her up and she was crushed against his chest. 'Darling girl, I cannot believe you have discovered this fact so soon. I realised I was irrevocably in love with you the day you proposed to me.'

His kiss was passionate and instead of being frightened by this, she responded. Only the return of the harassed outrider leading their horses prevented the inevitable conclusion to their embrace.

Kit tossed her into the saddle and remounted. 'Before you so rudely arrived and caused me to be thrown into the brambles, my love, I was looking down the lane for an exit from this field. We have missed our way by a considerable distance and are in danger of having no luncheon.'

'There is a clearing further back and the hedge is considerably lower at that point. We can jump out, can we not?'

He looked at her as if she was speaking in tongues. 'There might be room this side, sweetheart, but the lane is far too narrow to jump into. No, we must canter alongside until we find a way through.'

There was room for them to ride together and she could not help but notice he had not stopped to remove the leaves and cobwebs from his person before remounting. She wanted to laugh out loud, she was so happy she was in danger of bursting.

She thought him unmoved by the fact that they were now a genuine couple until he glanced across. His eyes blazed, leaving her in no doubt as to what he was thinking. 'Look, a gate just ahead.'

The detour they had been obliged to make meant a further two hours in the saddle, which normally she would not have objected to, but today all she could think of was what was going to take place in the privacy of their bedroom once they were alone. They had missed luncheon altogether as it was now late afternoon.

When they trotted into the courtyard of the inn they were to stay at the ostler who arrived to greet them seemed surprised. 'Good afternoon, sir, are you desirous of a reservation here?'

Kit swung to the cobbles. 'I am Lord Drake. Has the carriage with my servants and luggage not arrived? They were travelling several hours ahead of us and should have made arrangements.'

The man scratched his head. 'No, my lord, it ain't arrived. That's passing strange.'

She dismounted and moved to join

her husband. A flicker of unease ran through her, quelling her excitement and anticipation. He turned to his men, who were still mounted.

'Ride back along the road they would have taken. They must have suffered an accident of some sort. Discover what has taken place and then one of you return here and inform me.'

Both men clattered out of the yard. The landlord had been alerted of their arrival and came out bowing and nodding obsequiously.

'My lord, my lady, welcome to my humble establishment. I have my best chambers being made ready for you.'

The horses were led away and Kit offered her his arm. Before she took it she stretched up and removed the debris from his hair. 'There, you look more respectable. Shall we go in? I am sharp-set and would like to eat immediately.'

The landlord nodded and smiled some more. 'I shall have a repast sent up to your chambers immediately, my lady.'

A diminutive maidservant led them up the winding staircase and along a narrow, dark passageway. This was an ancient building and Kit would have to remember to lower his head to enter and exit any doorway if he did not wish to be knocked unconscious.

The rooms were no more than adequate, but the linen was clean and that was what mattered most. The girl left them and once the door was closed, he turned to her.

'Sweetheart, I shall eat with you but then must follow my men. Something catastrophic must have occurred for none of our servants to have managed to reach here.'

'There is another explanation, Kit, that has just occurred to me. This is not of the same high standard as the other places we have stayed — do you think there might be a second coaching inn called The Rising Sun in the neighbour-hood?'

He said something extremely impolite and then laughed. 'My wits are addled. I am certain that must be the case. However, we can hardly leave after so fulsome a welcome.'

9

Helena smiled. 'We certainly can. However, we had better wait and see if my surmise is correct.'

'That is easily solved. I shall go downstairs and ask the landlord if there is another establishment going under the same name.'

He was gone barely five minutes. 'The landlord was well aware we had made an error but had no intention of informing us. I have paid him as if we were remaining here, but our horses are being saddled as I speak.'

They were both mounted when one of his men cantered in. He was beaming. Kit raised a hand in salute and they trotted forward to meet him.

'We are at the wrong Rising Sun, are we not?'

'You are, my lord, it's no distance from here. They were equally anxious

171

and had sent out a search party for us.'

A mere half a mile later they entered a much more palatial yard where they were expected. The chambers were as good as any they had stayed in so far and the meal equally excellent.

Both she and Kit had asked for a bath to be drawn but had been told there was not sufficient water for two. 'In which case, darling girl, you bathe first and then I shall follow.'

'As you wish, my love.' Just the thought of him being naked in the same water she had used gave her palpitations. After her ablutions she donned a simple, high-waisted gown in the new, striped Indian cotton. It had no tiny buttons to undo, it just slipped over her head.

'Mary, the horses will need to rest tomorrow so we shall not be leaving here until the following day. This should give you ample time to catch up with the laundry. I shall send for you when I need you.'

The girl left with alacrity. The bath

had been positioned in his bedchamber — no doubt they assumed if there was only to be one bath it would be Kit who took it as he was the lord and master.

As soon as she was alone, she removed her gown and stepped out of her underpinnings before pulling it back on again. She was giddy with anticipation, not at all apprehensive, and wished he would be quick with his washing.

The splashing stopped. He was done — should she go to him or would he come in here? Not sure of the correct etiquette, she tapped on the communicating door and then stepped in.

Her breath caught in her throat. He was standing with his back to her with not a stitch of clothing on his magnificent frame. She had never seen a gentleman unclothed and had no idea that they were constructed so differently from her.

He remained with his back to her. 'Darling, do you intend to dither there, or come in? I thought I would be coming to you but I'm delighted to have you here instead.'

Her fingers gripped the door frame and heat travelled to a most unexpected place. She was incapable of answering. Then as he began to turn, she lost her courage and ran back to the safety of her chamber. Seeing him unclothed was not something she had anticipated. Did her parents do such a shocking thing? This doused her passion as nothing else could have.

* * *

In this room there were interior shutters that she had already pulled closed. The room was cool and dark, but not so dark one could not see perfectly. She wasn't sure if she should sit on the bed, sit in a chair — in fact she had no idea how these things proceeded. If she stood with her back to the door then she would not be alarmed or shocked if he wandered in as she had seen him a moment ago.

She was shivering, not sure if it was fear or something else that shook her. Then, as he had done once before, he was behind her without her realising he was in the room.

His arms encircled her and he drew her gently backwards so she was pressed against his body. He was no longer naked, and she was not sure if she was disappointed or relieved.

'Sweetheart, if you have changed your mind then we shall wait until you are ready to take this next step.' His warmth seeped into her and soon she was glowing all over.

'I wish to proceed. I was a little surprised to see you . . . to see you the way you were just now.'

'It is customary to remove one's garments — but if you are uncomfortable with this . . . '

'I am not. You have experience of bedroom matters, I am quite ignorant. I shall follow your lead.'

'In which case, darling girl, this can be removed.' He stepped back a few inches and grasped the hem of her gown and deftly took it off.

After that she forgot her reservations, forgot everything apart from the pleasure that becoming his true wife gave them both. Some hours later she woke to find him leaning on one elbow, watching her sleep.

'I cannot think why I was so against being your true wife, my love. I have never enjoyed anything so much as what we have been doing these past hours. All my mother told me, when I had my come-out, was that I must do my duty and not complain if a husband demanded his conjugal rights more than once a week.' She smiled at him, loving him even more, if that were possible. 'As I had no notion what conjugal rights were, it meant nothing to me. I should certainly complain if you only demanded them once or twice a week.'

His laugh echoed around the room. 'I can assure you, darling, that I shall be most attentive in that department.' His smile faded. 'You do understand that you could now be increasing? I have no intention of continuing with this trip if you become unwell.'

'Fiddlesticks to that! I have no desire to live under my parent's roof again and Audley Manor will not be ready for occupation until September, or so you said.'

He reached out and pushed a strand of hair from her forehead. 'Very well, but if you discover you are carrying my child then you will continue the journey in the carriage.'

She was about to protest but his eyes narrowed and she thought it better to acquiesce on this point. 'This will mean us travelling with our servants.'

His smile was teasing. 'No, my love, it will mean you travelling with our servants. I shall continue to ride.'

'Duncan can ride my horse so that you may have interesting business conversations that will be too complex and taxing for me to understand. I refuse to travel with a strange man in an enclosed carriage. I am perfectly content to do so with Mary, I have done so many times before.'

His hand was tracing patterns up and down her arm and his intent was obvious. She reached up and pulled him towards her and for the next hour all thought of carriages and passengers was forgotten. They fell asleep entwined and did not wake until full light.

When eventually she pulled the bell-strap, the time was embarrassingly late and she doubted they were still serving breakfast. Kit had returned to his own domain and she could hear him talking to his valet. The bed was mussed; no one could fail to know what had been taking place in it.

She tumbled out of bed and shrugged into her bedrobe just as there was a tap on the door heralding the arrival of her maid.

'I have hot water here, my lady, and your breakfast will be arriving in half an hour. It's ever so pretty around here. Are we to stop in Oxford next? I should dearly like to visit there.'

'I believe we are, and I am sure there will be an opportunity for you to look around when we arrive.' Mary was just pushing in the last pin when her husband called out from the sitting room that their breakfast had arrived.

The table was laden with appetising items from mushrooms, coddled eggs, slices of succulent pink ham, to fresh bread, butter and marmalade. She was delighted to see an enormous jug of coffee as this was her favourite beverage.

'You look enchanting, my love, is that the gown you were wearing last night?'

She blushed and nodded. 'It was on for such a short time I thought it acceptable to wear it today. This time I have on everything beneath it that I should.'

'I noticed that you do not wear a corset. My mother would be scandalised, but I am pleased. I cannot imagine that it is good for a lady to be so tightly laced she cannot breathe properly. You certainly could not ride safely wearing one.'

'Mama gave up the attempt to persuade me to adopt such an abomination. I am quite slender enough and have no need for one.'

'As far as I am concerned you are perfect from top to toe. As I am your lord and master, my opinion is the only one that counts. Are you sure you would not like another slice of ham on your plate? I believe there is a small corner you could squeeze it into.'

'I have a healthy appetite, as well you know, and this is both luncheon and breakfast so I am entitled to eat as much as I wish without being obliged to listen to sarcastic comments.'

'I cannot imagine how you remain the size you are if you eat as much as that at every meal.'

She slammed down her cutlery and fixed him with her fiercest stare. 'If you continue to comment on my meal you might well find yourself wearing it.'

He leaned back in his chair and

folded his arms. 'I do not recommend such an action, sweetheart. Childish behaviour will result in a suitably childish punishment.'

She had no doubt he meant a spanking — something she had received several of when she was little. 'In which case, my lord, pray excuse me. I shall eat no more. I am going for walk. I shall be accompanied by my maid so you may remain here and finish your meal.'

'I apologise, sweetheart, I shall refrain from teasing you. Please resume your seat and finish your repast.'

It would have been churlish to ignore his plea when he was being so pleasant. She sat down and soon they were munching together in silence and did not speak until their plates were cleared.

'That was delicious. I am now going for that walk around the town. Do you wish to accompany me?'

'No, sweetheart, I have business to attend to. Remember to take your maid with you.'

She stuck out her tongue at him and he chuckled. 'You are a baggage, my love, and I love you for it.'

'And I love you for your irascible temper and bullying manners.'

She skipped hastily into her own bedchamber and was relieved to find Mary there. 'I need my bonnet, reticule and walking boots, as do you. We are going to explore the town.'

*   *   *

Kit had no wish to worry her, but the man he had sent with the letter to her parents had yet to return despite the fact that they had remained in the same place for so long. He was anxious to see if Joe, Bill's younger brother, had now returned.

He found the three men gathered at the far side of the stable yard. They looked relieved to see him. 'I take it that your brother has not reappeared from his errand.'

'No, my lord, he ain't and we're

right worried about it too. Somethink untoward has happened to him. We was discussing whether one of us should . . . '

'Absolutely not. I shall write to the earl and make enquiries. It would be better if they investigated from their end. I do not think there is any need to worry unduly at present as any number of trivial incidents could have delayed him.'

'Right enough, sir. We was paid to protect you and her ladyship and we can't do that if we ain't here.'

Kit was about to correct this erroneous assumption but something made him hesitate. The hairs on the back of his neck stood to attention. Was the continued absence of Joe in some way connected to the men making enquiries about himself?

'We shall leave here early tomorrow so, Ed, you must accompany the carriage. This means you will be departing at dawn. Bill, you and Sam will ride with us as usual.'

He went in search of his manservant, Duncan, and explained his concerns. 'I think it is wise, my lord, to be cautious in the circumstances. The coachman and his assistant are armed, as am I. That young man, Ed, can use a cudgel and his fists, but he doesn't carry weapons.'

'Then I am satisfied that we will come to no harm. I believe we are thinking the same thing — that if someone is looking for me then they would assume I was inside the carriage and might well attack that.'

'I was wondering, sir, if it might be better to travel as one party for the next few days. That way there will be six armed men and no one would attack so large a group.'

'That is an excellent suggestion. I shall leave it to you to inform the men. We shall all depart together at eight o'clock tomorrow morning.'

Now he had voiced his worries, he was not happy about Helena being out alone. He was about to go in search of her when she hailed him from the other side of the road. He hid his smile and tried to look stern as her shout had turned several heads.

'My lord, have you decided to come with me? I am told there is a watermill we can visit no more than a mile from here.'

There were no vehicles trundling past so he strode across. 'Kindly refrain from yelling like a fishwife, my dear, it is not becoming of you and inappropriate for the wife of someone as high in the instep as myself.'

She giggled and put her hand through his arm exactly where it belonged. Her maid was hovering anxiously behind them. He raised an eyebrow and Helena gave him permission to dismiss her.

The watermill was mildly interesting, but he enjoyed every moment of the stroll because he was in her company. They had talked of this and that but he had yet to inform her of the change of plans. He was reluctant to spoil her happy mood.

'Kit, something is troubling you. Tell me, I do not like to see you like this.'

She was more observant than he had realised. 'My love, the man I sent with your letter has failed to return. There is probably nothing to worry about, but to be sure, we are travelling as one party until he rejoins us.'

'That makes perfect sense to me. I think if I travelled in the coach and Duncan took my horse that would make things even safer. As you know, I am a competent shot and could protect both Mary and I in the event of an attack.'

'Are you telling me, in a roundabout way, that you carry a pistol with you?'

'I have one in my reticule — I believe it sensible to be prepared for any eventuality.'

He thought he knew her, but every day he was learning something else. 'First Duncan and now you have suggested a way forward that I should have thought of myself.' He quickly glanced around and they were alone on the towpath. 'My wits are befuddled, darling, since discovering that you return my feelings.'

Their embrace was disturbed by the arrival of a wet, shaggy dog eager to join in the fun. By the time they had sent him on his way they were both sadly mired. She viewed her ruined gown and he waited for an outburst.

'Look at this. I do hope anyone seeing us so dishevelled will not decide we have been misbehaving in the countryside.'

He kissed her again and then, hand in hand, they returned to the inn. It was hard to be anything but happy when in her company.

★ ★ ★

Kit left her bed in order to avoid giving Mary a fit of the vapours on finding him naked beneath the covers. He had been open about his concerns, and she appreciated being treated with such respect. Being cooped up in a carriage was a small sacrifice to make in order to ensure the best possible arrangements had been made to keep them all from harm.

After a light breakfast, no time for anything substantial, and far too early to expect the kitchen to have freshly baked goods ready for consumption, they made their way to the waiting carriage. The three outriders and Duncan were already mounted, and Kit's horse was stamping impatiently, awaiting his owner.

'We will stop for luncheon, but not before. As we discussed, I have altered our route so that we will not be travelling in the same direction as you stated in your letter.'

'I care not where we go, as long as we are together. If we have to return, then so be it. I'm resigned to having to reside in the familial home once more.'

'It might be the best solution, but we will press on until we hear from your father.' His lips were warm and hard on hers and she smiled at the shocked gasp coming from inside the carriage. 'This is not what I planned for you, sweetheart. I hope you will not be too bored, shut up in here after the excitement of galloping all over the countryside with me.'

He lifted her into the carriage, his hands warm around her waist. 'I shall imagine myself the heroine of a romance novel, being pursued by a dastardly villain. You are the brave knight escorting me to my destination.'

'I should prefer to be your handsome, courageous husband protecting you from . . . from whatever danger might be lurking in the undergrowth.'

She was still smiling when she settled onto the squabs. The thought that there might be anything lurking in the undergrowth apart from rabbits and voles was an amusing idea.

There was no need to wear her bonnet inside the vehicle so she untied the ribbons and handed it to Mary. Then she swung her feet up, arranged the cushions behind her head, and prepared to sleep. There had been little of that for either her or her husband last night. He was made of sterner stuff than she, being a man, and no doubt would remain alert until tonight.

'I am going to rest my eyes, Mary, please wake me if there is anything interesting to see from the windows.'

However hard she tried, she could not settle. The interior of the carriage was stifling and the constant jouncing and jolting meant she was obliged to constantly snatch at the leather strap in order to keep herself on the seat.

'We need to let down the windows, Mary. I shall do this one and you do the other.'

'My lady, if we do so we will both be covered in dust.'

'I should prefer that than to be roasted alive.'

It took her a few moments to release the leather strap from its metal peg and move the glass. Immediately a welcome gust of air flowed in and she sat back, satisfied she had made the right decision. With both windows open soon she was feeling more the thing.

10

Helena had scarcely settled back when she heard Kit shout a command to the coachman. Then the carriage was suddenly rattling along at a canter. Why were they travelling at such speed? Without stopping to think, she poked her head out of the window in the hope of seeing what was causing them to travel so fast.

Kit must have seen her; her hair was bright enough to be visible from a distance. He arrived beside the window. He was obliged to shout over the rattling and clattering of the wheels. 'This is a deserted stretch of road, there have been several incidents of highway robbery along this stretch over the past few months. I thought it better to push the team and rest them later.'

'I understand. Take care, my love.'

He vanished from sight and she

dropped back onto the squabs, pressing her back against the side of the carriage and taking a firm grip on the strap.

Her maid was similarly employed. Helena could not seriously consider the notion that they were in any danger from footpads, highwaymen, or anyone else. Kit knew what he was about and would not put her through this discomfort, not to mention the likelihood of the carriage overturning when travelling at this speed, unless he had good reason.

Both she and her companion were nauseous when the mad dash finally ended. The carriage did not just drop to a walking pace but halted altogether. The door swung open and he reached in and lifted her out. She had never been more grateful to have her feet on firm ground than she was at that moment.

'We shall rest here for a while; the horses are blown, they need time to recover.'

The place they had stopped was an

open stretch of road with no ditches or trees for villains to hide behind and within sight of a substantial dwelling and several smaller cottages, which presumably were to house the workers associated with this estate.

The coachman had driven them to the side of the road where they were visible from both directions and there was ample room for any other vehicle to pass. That this place was also on a slight rise and allowed those upon it to be able to see anyone approaching made a flicker of unease run through her.

'Something has happened. I can see from the way you have positioned the men and the fact that they have their weapons to hand that you are expecting trouble. Please tell me what is happening.'

'We are being followed. Duncan saw four men, their faces obscured, travelling at speed a mile or two behind us. This is a real threat; I have no idea why anyone should wish us harm, but I thank God I am prepared for their attack.'

'What do you wish me to do?'

Her calm acceptance of this hideous news pleased him. He threw his arm around her shoulders and drew her close. 'You will not like what I am suggesting, sweetheart, but the safest place for you and your maid is under the carriage. Duncan has put a blanket there so you will not be obliged to lie on the dirt.'

'Good heavens, Kit, do you think me so feeble-spirited that I would object to anything at all that you suggest in the circumstances?'

Bill was standing in his stirrups, staring down the road. He raised a hand. It was obviously the signal to say that the would-be attackers were close. She didn't need telling to dash to the carriage. Mary was already wriggling underneath; Duncan had obviously explained to her why they had to do this.

Once they were safely behind the

wheels, Helena removed her small pistol from her reticule, checked it was primed and loaded, and put it down within easy reach. She only had one shot, but if needs be she would make it count.

★ ★ ★

Kit had no military experience but he hoped he had positioned his men at the most strategic points: two were twenty yards ahead of the carriage and there was one on either side of the road. He and Duncan remained where they were easily seen by the approaching men, the idea being that as soon as the would-be attackers were surrounded, they would be the ones attacked.

It occurred to him belatedly that if one of them had a rifle, they could shoot him without coming close enough to be apprehended. 'Dismount, do it now, get your head below the horizon.'

As he rolled from the saddle, a bullet whistled past, missing him by inches. If he had been on his stallion he would be dead. Whoever these men were, they were not here to abduct him. They were here to kill him.

A fusillade of shots followed, keeping him flattened beneath his horse's hoofs. He was in more danger of being trampled than being hit, but he daren't move. The silence was profound. The riflemen must be reloading.

Then the air was split by the sound of muskets — his men were returning fire. They wouldn't hit anyone as the range of their guns was much less than a rifle, but at least it would demonstrate they were armed and ready to fight.

'Stay where you are, Helena, you will be safe under there.'

'This is probably not the time to point out that perhaps stopping on the brow of the hill was not the best policy, in the circumstances.'

'I am fully aware of my error of judgement, my dear, but so kind of you to mention it.'

He heard her laughing and his mouth

curved. Whoever these brigands were, they would not succeed. He had everything to live for, and they would rue the day they had attacked him and his beloved.

'My lord, the gunshots must have been heard at the house. There's half a dozen mounted men galloping to our assistance.'

This was the worst possible news. His would-be rescuers would be easy targets when they emerged onto the road and he had no intention of allowing innocent people to be killed on his behalf. Without a second thought he scrambled to his knees and then, in a crouched position, scuttled like a beetle to the other side of the road. He then dived head first over the low hedge and into the comparative safety of the field beyond.

He surged to his feet and ran, shouting and waving, towards the approaching horsemen. They immediately changed course and thundered towards him. When they were in hailing distance, he yelled a warning.

'Riflemen, take cover.'

To his astonishment, they swerved back onto their original path and continued, now with a motley selection of swords held roughly in a cavalry charge position, towards the hiding place of the shooters. He stood up, sure he was safe as the riflemen would be concentrating on the horsemen, and then ran back to the carriage.

There were a further two gunshots, a lot of yelling and then he heard at least one of the horsemen cantering back towards his party. He leaned down and pulled Helena to her feet.

A young man about his own age dismounted from his sweating horse and strode forward. 'Captain Forsyth, at your service. We routed the blighters. I've sent my men after them but I doubt we'll have much luck. They were skirmishers; they can blend into the landscape better than any soldiers I know.'

Kit stepped forward and offered his

hand. It was shaken vigorously. 'Lord Christopher Drake, delighted to make your acquaintance. This is my wife, Lady Helena.'

Instead of curtsying, she also offered her hand and the captain shook it. 'Thank you for coming to our aid so speedily. We were pinned down, you know, by expert marksmen.'

'A havey-cavey business, my lady. Most upsetting for you. Might I suggest that you return with me to my home where my mother, Lady Forsyth, will make you most welcome.'

She looked for permission before replying. 'We should love to. We are not safe on the open road with those villains still out there.'

* * *

Kit escorted her to the carriage. 'I am quite bewildered by the sudden arrival of those men. How can he be a captain if he is not wearing a uniform?'

'I care not, sweetheart, their arrival

saved us from an unpleasant situation. I was not unduly worried as long as we could stop the riflemen from approaching any closer. There was bound to be another coach or carriage along this road. They could hardly continue to fire at us under those circumstances.'

'Captain Forsyth, if he is indeed a genuine captain, obviously has some military experience as he recognised our attackers as being skirmishers. This makes them all the more dangerous, especially as we are now certain they wish to kill you for some inexplicable reason.'

He lifted her in and she was pleased to see Mary already there, looking remarkably calm after spending half an hour under a carriage.

'Although I am unsure about accepting an invitation to the house of someone we know nothing about, Helena, I agree with you that it would be foolhardy to continue as things are.'

He slammed the door shut and she watched him jog across to his horse and swing into the saddle in one smooth movement without recourse to the stirrup iron for assistance. She explained to Mary of their change of plans and her maid nodded.

'Mr Duncan told me we were invited to visit with Lady Forsyth. We will be safer there than travelling along the road like this. Mr Duncan thinks that the captain maybe leads the local militia and is not a member of the regular army.'

She hid her smile behind her hand. From the frequent use of Duncan's name Mary was beginning to view the valet in a romantic way. He was perhaps a little old for her maid, he must be over thirty, but he was a handsome fellow, intelligent, and what could be better than her abigail and his valet being married to each other?

Of course, if Mary were to be in an interesting condition the girl would be obliged to leave her service and they had become close over the years they had been together.

Why was she thinking about such things when not half an hour ago Kit had almost been murdered before her eyes? It was as if she had swallowed a large stone. If anything were to happen to her husband she would be destroyed. It had not been her intention to fall in love with him, to fall in love with anyone, but too late to repine. She placed her hand protectively across her stomach. Was it possible she was already carrying their first child?

It mattered not that they were going to a stranger's establishment, they would be safe there, especially as the captain appeared to have half a dozen men at his disposal. She would have to write to Theo immediately and ask him to bring the local militia to escort them back to safety. There was no possibility of them continuing on their journey after today.

The carriage halted in front of the steps and a smiling, plump, middle-aged woman, dressed like a lady half her age, was at the window waving to them as if they were already known to her.

A footman opened the door and dropped the steps so she could climb out. Kit arrived at her side and offered his arm, which she took gratefully. For some reason her legs were shaking and she needed his support.

Before she could protest he swept her into his arms. 'You don't look at all well, my love. I thought you had taken my near demise too calmly.'

She rested her head on his shoulder and let the world swirl around her head, glad she didn't have to make a curtsy to their hostess when she was feeling so peculiar.

★   ★   ★

She awoke to find herself in her nightgown with her beloved stretched out beside her, watching her anxiously. He had at least removed his boots and topcoat which, in the circumstances, she supposed was acceptable.

'I am perfectly well, my love. A combination of too much excitement and too little sleep. I am fully recovered now.' His eyes darkened and she laughed and raised a hand. 'No, not that recovered. I wish to get up immediately and speak to Lady Forsyth. She must think me a poor specimen indeed to have fainted quite away like that.'

'She thinks, sweetheart, that you are a well-bred young lady reacting as one would expect to appalling circumstances. You have been asleep for three hours and I have been beside you all that time so have yet to discover exactly who we are residing with.'

'Then you had better ask Duncan, he will have discovered everything we wish to know by now. Did you write to Theo? I thought we had better curtail our wedding trip and return immediately to the safety of Faulkner Court. I assume that you had already decided the same thing.'

He leaned down and pressed a firm

kiss on her parted lips. 'I had, but was reluctant to give you the bad news as you were so eager to visit the north of England. I need to discover who is behind this attack and cannot do so until we are back.'

'Would you like me to help you get dressed, my love?' His smile was wicked and she giggled and waved him away.

With Mary's help she was soon suitably attired in a smart afternoon gown of fine cotton with a golden hue, and daffodil yellow embroidery around the hem, neckline and sleeves. Her hair had been arranged simply, in a coronet of braids around her head.

The communicating door to Kit's room remained open and she strolled through to find it empty. She walked through into the sitting room, but that too was deserted.

He could not be far away as he was well aware how quickly she could get dressed. She wandered back into his room and then heard male voices coming from behind the wall. How strange! She put her ear to the panelling but the words were muffled and she could not make out who was speaking or what they were saying. Then she discovered there was a hidden door for the servants to use.

She pushed it open and was about to call out when the subject they were discussing stopped the words in her throat. Duncan was speaking, presumably to Kit.

'My lord, Forsyth isn't a captain of anything apart from his own retainers. From what I have garnered downstairs the young man is a trifle unsteady, wanted to buy his colours but was turned down as being unfit for duty. Sir James, his pa, died last year. He had kept his son's instability in check, but Lady Forsyth dotes on him and does nothing to curb his wildness and delusions.'

'I cannot see that this is a problem to us as we are only here until our own men arrive to escort us home.'

'Coming to our rescue has tipped

him into mania. He has decided to hunt down those men himself.'

She could remain hidden no longer as eavesdropping on a conversation was the height of bad manners. She cleared her throat loudly. 'Kit, I think that this is something I need to be privy to before we go downstairs.' The two of them stepped through the door and joined her in the sitting room. 'I heard that our host is mad and imagines himself a captain in the army and has now gone to hunt down the assassins. Is this not a good thing as far as we are concerned?'

'No, sweetheart, it is a disaster. The men he leads are outside workers, they gallop about behind him waving a sword with no notion how to use it or any desire to do so. All of them could be killed and it will be my fault . . . '

'It certainly will not. You can hardly be blamed for that poor young man believing he is a soldier. Neither can you be blamed for having several riflemen trying to shoot you.'

'You are splitting hairs, my dear. You know very well that it is my presence here that has put Sir Robert in deadly peril. A letter has already gone to your brother, but this time it will travel by express and not with one of my men.'

From the sadness in his eyes she realised he thought Joe had been ambushed and was probably lying dead in a ditch somewhere. She prayed he was wrong. Two days ago she had been the happiest girl in the kingdom and now everything was changed.

'There is nothing you can do about it until you discover who is behind it. What have you told Lady Forsyth?'

'Duncan has spoken with her and said that they were opportunist foot-pads, ex-soldiers using their military skills for nefarious reasons.'

'She must be beside herself having her beloved son putting his life at risk in this way.'

'That I cannot attest to. Shall we go down and speak to her ourselves?'

The stairs lead to a spacious entrance hall with a black and white chequered floor which she much admired. There was a liveried footman standing to attention to the left of the front door. This must be a wealthy household indeed to have a servant standing about on the off-chance somebody might knock on the door.

Double doors stood open and from her vantage point halfway down the staircase she could see into the chamber. This was the main reception room, and there was the soft murmur of female voices drifting from it.

'The household appears calm so perhaps we are worrying unnecessarily.'

He nodded. 'I hope you are correct, my love. There is obviously more than one lady residing here.'

The footman moved as if stuck by a pin and leaped to intercept them. Kit only just avoided walking into the wretched man.

'Lord and Lady Drake,' the man yelled, causing her to miss her footing and step on the hem of her gown.

Kit's prompt action prevented her from a fall. He glared at the servant but the man ignored him and returned to his previous position. They had no option but to enter, as they had been announced so loudly.

The two ladies sitting by the open French doors continued to converse as if they were invisible. An inappropriate desire to giggle almost overwhelmed her. He grinned. 'It would seem we have stepped into a madhouse, sweetheart. Unless both ladies are stone deaf.'

'Shall we wave, try and attract their attention, or just go in?'

He marched forward, taking her with him They were halfway down the drawing room when Lady Forsyth looked up. 'I am glad to see you looking fully restored, my lady. Forgive me for not standing, or greeting you when you came in. I am rather deaf.'

Helena exchanged a glance with Kit. Why a lack of hearing should prevent a person from standing was a mystery to her.

'Thank you for taking us in, my lady. I hope my wife and I shall not be obliged to disturb your household for more than a day or two.'

Helena tried not to laugh. Kit had spoken so loudly he had scared doves from the terrace outside the window. The elderly lady, presumably a companion, looked at them with interest, but said nothing.

Lady Forsyth waved to a daybed close by. 'Please be seated, sir, I cannot abide a gentleman who looms over one.'

There was a choking sound from him and she dare not catch his eye. Once they were both settled Kit boomed another remark. 'Has Sir Robert returned from his chase? He would do better to leave this matter to the local militia.'

'My son believes he is the militia, my lord. He will come to no harm, I assure you. He will gallop about the place waving his sword and then return satisfied he's done his job.' She beamed at them. 'I cannot thank you enough for allowing my boy to act out his fantasy on your behalf.'

Strangely, the lady did not speak loudly herself, as one would have expected when a person was very hard of hearing. Kit was about to shout a reply but she squeezed his arm. 'No, please not again. Please use your normal voice.'

He raised an eyebrow but did as she suggested. 'We have not been introduced to your companion, my lady.'

'I am Miss Veronica Forsyth, aunt to that silly boy and sister-in-law to Lady Forsyth. Robert might be unbalanced but he is not truly mad. He will not go near enough to those who attempted to rob you to be shot — even if by some miracle he came across them.'

'Thank you, I should not wish anyone to be injured on my account.'

Lady Forsyth got up and, without bidding them farewell, sailed down the chamber and vanished into the hall. This was a household of eccentrics and Helena thought they might be safer travelling than remaining where they were.

'I apologise for her poor manners. I fear she too is becoming unbalanced. Unfortunately, this taint is in the family on her side. She has an uncle and a sister incarcerated in an asylum.'

'We shall not remain here; our presence has disturbed your sister-in-law and your nephew and the sooner we leave the better. Our horses will be rested and my wife has now fully recovered from the shock.'

Helena had thought Miss Forsyth might protest at their sudden departure but instead she looked relieved. 'I had not liked to suggest it, but it would be best if you departed immediately.' She stood and curtsied. Kit nodded and she did the same.

11

Helena and Kit hurried from the room, eager to be away from this unsettling establishment. 'The luggage was not brought in, Mary only has to pack my night things and I shall be ready.'

'I shall get the carriage harnessed and round up the men.' He rested his hand on her shoulder for a moment. 'We will remain on the toll road and travel as speedily as possible. With luck, Theo will meet us tomorrow with further protection.'

'Do you think we are still in danger of being attacked? Surely, whoever it was will assume we are staying here overnight at the very least and will not expect us to leave so precipitously.'

'Sir Robert might be touched in the attic, but he was correct in his assumption that these men have been professional soldiers. They will discover we have gone and set out after us, possibly within an hour or two.'

She picked up her skirts and ran back to the chamber she had occupied so briefly. 'Mary, we are leaving immediately.'

'Yes, my lady, I have already packed. Mr Duncan thought his lordship would not wish to linger here.'

Together they ran back through the house, startling the footman for a second time. Despite his shock at her unruly behaviour, he managed to have the front door open as they arrived.

She had been only a few minutes yet the carriage was outside, the three men mounted and Duncan and Kit also ready to vault into the saddle. Less than ten minutes from their interview with the lady of the house, the carriage was speeding down the driveway flanked by the five men.

They travelled for two hours without pause, but not at breakneck speed, so the horses were not blown. Their first halt was at a busy coaching inn. Kit opened the door and lifted her out.

'We shall eat, allow the horses to recuperate, and then continue until dark. There's been no sign of pursuit, but that does not mean they will not catch up with us.'

'Where are we going to sleep tonight? It is already seven o'clock and will be dark in a few hours.'

His lips tightened as if irritated by her queries. 'I am well aware of the time, Helena, and reservations will have been made by the time we wish to stop.'

'I shall not apologise for enquiring, I am entitled to know what is going on. If you had wanted a submissive and silent wife you should have married someone else.' This was a silly thing to say, but her nerves were jangled as she had spent the past two hours expecting to hear rifle shots at any moment.

'Indeed I should have. You are pointing out the obvious, madam.'

For a dreadful moment she thought him in earnest, but then his smile told her he was teasing. 'I thought I should like to lead an exciting life and travel about the place, but I find I am not enjoying this at all. I should be braver, but all I can think is that at any moment you could be killed and my life would be over too.'

'Would you be more comfortable if I travelled inside with you?'

A weight lifted from her chest. 'Yes, I would be happier having you beside me. What will happen to your stallion as I know that he does not like to be led?'

'The under-coachman is an excellent horseman so he can ride him. There was no time to arrange for refreshments so I hope this place can accommodate us.'

In fact their repast was palatable, the facilities acceptable and within three quarters of an hour they were ready to depart once more. The interior of the carriage was now gloomy as the sun was setting and Mary made herself invisible in the corner, leaving them to sit side by side opposite her.

Obviously, they could not converse

freely. Instead she leaned against his shoulder, he put his arm around her waist and they both dozed. She didn't awake until they arrived at their overnight stop.

The chamber they were allocated was small but the bedlinen was fresh and smelt of lavender and that was all she cared about. When they were making love she was able to forget about the dangers lurking outside and rejoice in the fact that she was married to a man she loved to distraction. He left her in no doubt he reciprocated her feelings in full.

* * *

Kit waited until his beloved was asleep and then slipped out from under the sheet and dressed in the darkness. He placed the letter he had written earlier on the pillow along with a cloth purse filled with golden guineas.

Duncan was awaiting him in the coach yard, as were the other three men. The carriage horses stamped and shook their heads, the noise loud in the darkness.

'Are the horses capable of travelling at speed until morning?'

'They are, my lord, but, forgive me for speaking out of turn; are you quite sure you wish to deliberately draw these men after you?' Duncan asked.

'My wife is in danger as long as she is with me, by doing this I can be sure she will be safe. They will follow believing we are both inside the vehicle.'

He had no doubt he was doing the right thing by abandoning Helena at this inn. She would not be best pleased, but she would be safe and that was all that mattered to him. He would willingly give his life if it meant she would remain unharmed.

They clattered out of the yard and set off towards Faulkner Court. The under-coachman was travelling inside and he had borrowed the man's topcoat. His plan was to fool those following him into believing that he was inside the carriage.

Knowing his brother-in-law as he did, he was certain Theo would ride all night too. He was hopeful they would rendezvous before morning and could reverse matters by pursuing the pursuers. He would not return for Helena until he was certain matters were settled and she would be safe.

There was no sign of anything untoward for the remainder of the night and at dawn he was confident they were in no danger. He indicated to the coachman to turn into the hostelry they were approaching.

The horses required at least four hours' respite before they would be fit to continue, possibly longer. His men could eat and then sleep — he was sure they wouldn't mind using the stables just this once. He hoped there would be a chamber available for him and Duncan.

Breakfast was excellent and he was about to make his way to the room he had been allocated when there was a clatter of hooves on the cobbles outside. His man had been standing, alert, at the window and he turned with a broad smile.

'It's Lord Faulkner and a dozen men just arrived, sir. You were right to think they would choose this place.'

Kit greeted his friend with open arms. 'I cannot tell you how pleased I am to see you, Theo.'

'And I you. Is my sister asleep?'

'She is not with me, I left her somewhere she will be out of harm's way. She will be furious with me, but better that than having her at risk. They serve a good breakfast here, I have eaten but I will join you. I wish to know if you have discovered who is behind these attacks.'

Theo was looking at him strangely. 'I know who is behind this — it is your cousin. It would appear that you are now the Duke of Andover. Your father was the eldest son and changed places with his twin in order to marry your mother.'

For a second, Kit was unable to process this news. 'How did you learn this extraordinary information?'

'The details were in a box locked away in the attic of your home. Lady Drake knew of this box but had never thought to look inside. She said that if your father had wished her to know he would have shown her the contents.'

'It all makes sense now. My cousin must have grown up with the expectation of being the next duke. In his position I should have been shocked, but I would not have attempted to murder the true heir.'

'I think you made the right decision leaving Helena behind. My horses and men require rest and then we can go to your ancestral home and confront this madman.' Theo rubbed his stubbly face. 'I need a shave and a change of shirt, but first I must eat. Your lawyers are now aware of your change of circumstances and will be putting an announcement in The Times today.

'Do you think that will be enough for

the riflemen to give up? After all, their employer can never claim the title now.'

Theo slammed his hand against the wall. 'My God, Helena could be in deadly danger. Your cousin remains your heir if you die. He will think that there is a possibility my sister could be in an interesting condition . . . '

'She might well be. It is now a true marriage, with deep and abiding love on both sides, so do not look so disapproving.'

Kit's meal threatened to return. He swallowed and took several deep breaths. Disaster averted. 'I cannot believe I have put her in more danger. I only arrived here a short while ago so my mounts are not fit to travel. I shall hire a horse, if they have one up to my weight.'

'Whilst you try and find us horses, I shall grab something to eat. Your men and mine can follow as soon as they can do so without danger to themselves or the horses.'

Duncan, as always, had been at his

side during this conversation. 'I'll find us something suitable, your grace, and explain the situation to the men.'

He raised a hand to acknowledge this suggestion and then followed Theo inside. Whilst his friend rapidly consumed an enormous plate of cold cuts, pickles and bread, he told him what had transpired so far. Despite the dire circumstances, his companion laughed when he heard about the Forsyths.

'It would seem that you are surrounded by madness, Kit — do you wish me to address you as your grace in future?'

'I'll draw your cork if you do so. Hell's teeth! A week ago I was a lord in want of funds and now I am a duke. Am I still in want of funds, I wonder?'

'From what I gathered you are fabulously wealthy. If you wish to, you can return the settlement — I'm sure that Papa would not refuse to take it.'

'My head is spinning at the implications. Exactly where is this Andover Hall?'

'Hertfordshire, adjacent to St Albans.' His friend tossed down his cutlery, wiped his mouth with a napkin and drained his mug of porter. 'I am done. Shall we depart? How long do you think it will take us?'

'Across the fields at a gallop, half the time it took to get here. Two or three hours, no more than that.'

Duncan had worked miracles in his absence: saddled and waiting were three enormous hunters, more than adequate for the purpose.

'I beg your pardon, your grace, but I was obliged to purchase these animals. I had not the wherewithal to pay but they were happy to accept my vow when they understood I was the man of affairs to the Duke of Andover.'

'Good man, the owners will be well-recompensed when this is over.'

The three of them left the coach yard at a decorous pace — the road was too busy to do anything else. Kit led them past the church and into the open fields beyond. He kicked his massive gelding into a gallop and the other two followed suit. He prayed they were wrong in their assumptions and that when he arrived, Helena would be there to greet him.

★ ★ ★

Something woke Helena at dawn and she sat up with a jolt to find the space beside her not only empty but cold. Her questing fingers touched two objects — one a purse with several coins in it and the other a letter of some sort.

'Mary, I need a candle . . . ' There was no response because, of course, her maid was sleeping elsewhere. She rolled out of bed, stubbing her toe painfully in the darkness, and found her way to the window. She pulled back the curtains and there was just enough light for her to be able to peruse the letter.

My darling,
I hope you will forgive me
abandoning you like this. My

intention is to keep you safe from harm at all costs. The villains will assume we are both in the carriage and follow us.

I'm sorry but you must remain where you are until I come back for you. I'm hopeful I shall meet up with Theo on the road and together we can settle this matter.

I love you and hope you will still love me when I return.

The handwriting was fierce and dark like him. How could he abandon her in this dismal place and without even a change of clothes? The trunks would have had to be left attached to the rear of the carriage if his deception was to work.

There was sufficient water in the jug for her to complete her morning ablutions. The ensemble she had been wearing yesterday was not irredeemably crumpled and would do very well for today. However, if her errant husband failed to return the following day she would have something very caustic to say on the matter when he eventually returned.

Strangely, she was not angry at his desertion. She was concerned for his safety, and for that of her brother, because his mention of settling this matter could only mean one thing — that he intended to find the man behind this outrage and put an end to it. This could well be a dangerous enterprise. She sent a fervent prayer to the Almighty that he would come to no harm, and neither would Theo. Hastily, she added further words asking that the men with him should also remain unscathed.

There was nothing to read in this small chamber and as she paced the room she came to a decision. One that she was quite certain her husband would disapprove of, but as he was not here, he had nothing to say on the matter.

She had no idea of the time. The sun was just coming up so it must be around four o'clock in the morning, perhaps a little later. Small wonder the place was quiet. She checked the contents of the cloth bag and was delighted to find ten guineas inside. This was more than enough to pay her reckoning and purchase two seats on a coach to London. From there it would be simple enough to obtain further tickets to take her home to Faulkner Court.

After a further tedious wait there was movement in the stable yard as the ostlers and grooms went about their business. With luck, Mary would come to her soon. No sooner had the thought entered her head than there was a knock on the door. She ran to open it and was delighted to see the girl carrying her breakfast.

'Come in. We have been abandoned, Mary, but I do not intend to remain here. As soon as we have broken our fast I need you to find me a conveyance of some sort to take me to the nearest coaching inn. We shall return by common stage. We might have to stay overnight in London, but I am sure we can manage that. My only dilemma is that I have no luggage at all . . . '

'No, my lady, that is incorrect. Mr Duncan left your small trunk and my valise outside my chamber door. Some-one is bringing it here right now.' The girl put down the tray and went to usher in a boot boy carrying the smallest of the trunks.

'Put it there, if you please. Lady Drake requires a chaise to be outside in half an hour. I shall be downstairs soon to settle our account.'

The boy tugged his forelock and trotted off. Having luggage meant that they would be less conspicuous than if they were without baggage — however — as far as she recalled, the contents of the trunk would be of little use to her as it held only toiletries, stationery and other such items.

Mary saw her expression and smiled. 'I thought the same when I saw it, my lady, but would you believe, it has everything we need for the next few days.'

'That is good news. Join me at the table, there is no time to stand on ceremony this morning. The sooner we leave the sooner we shall be back. Lord Drake could well be delayed for several days and I have no intention of remaining here for that length of time.'

She had little appetite but her maid tucked in with enthusiasm. Pen, ink and paper might well have been removed from the trunk but she hoped not. There was no paper but the inkpot and a selection of pens remained snugly in the compartment in the lid.

She quickly penned a note on the bottom of the one he had left her.

Dearest Kit,
I could not possibly stay here and wait for you so shall catch the stage and return home. I apologise that you have had a wasted journey to collect me.
I am certain you will be angrier

with me for my actions than I was with you.

She signed it with a flourish. She managed to melt the wax blob on the back and resealed it. 'Mary, if you have finished we must leave. I believe we can manage the trunk and the bag between us without the necessity of recalling the boy to help us.'

The narrow stairs were tricky to negotiate but they did so without mishap. Mary delivered the letter and after a lively discussion appeared satisfied with the reckoning. This time there was someone to carry the trunk and the bag out to the waiting chaise.

'These can come in with us, there is no need to tie them on the back for so short a journey.'

The driver snapped his whip and the vehicle moved forward smoothly — well as smoothly as any carriage can over cobbles.

'Mary, do you know how far away from here the coaching inn is?'

'It is no more than a mile, so the landlord told me. He also said there was a coach leaving at eight o'clock and we should be in good time for that.'

'Excellent, we shall just have to hope all the inside seats are not reserved.'

12

Kit was forced to slow down their breakneck speed as all three horses were almost on their knees. However urgent the reason, he would not kill his mount. His face was mud-streaked, his clothes no better and his companions were in a similar state.

Theo came alongside. 'How much further is it, do you think?'

'See that church steeple in the distance — that is our destination. We must walk the horses from here. In fact, I suggest that we dismount and lead them. Loosen their girths, allow them to recover.'

'I reckon it to be about two miles to the inn, your grace. We shall be there within the hour even travelling at this pace.'

They were all too exhausted for idle chatter. He tried to convince himself that the extra time would make no difference to the outcome, but he was not sanguine they would be in time. If his cousin was truly bent on removing all obstacles to his title, regardless of the outcome to himself, then they could already be several hours too late. Taking Helena would ensure they could also take himself.

The ostler recognised him and hurried to take the horses. 'They are cool enough to drink; take good care of them, for they have served us well.'

He led the way into the cramped vestibule and the landlord beamed and rushed forward, waving the letter he had left Helena. His name had been scribbled on the front. He took it outside to open — it was far too dark inside to be able to read anything.

'Good God! She and her girl left here at dawn to catch the stagecoach to London from the coaching inn further down the road.' There was a stable-hand sweeping in the corner and he beckoned him over. 'How did Lady

Drake travel to catch the stage? Did you see her leave?'

The boy grinned. 'I did that, my lord. The master borrowed a chaise from a guest and it delivered her right enough. He waited and saw her onto the coach before he returned.'

Kit was so relieved he tossed the urchin a silver sixpence for the information. Theo and Duncan had overheard this conversation. 'Thank the good Lord for that. Duncan, see if you can find us beds, a bath and something to eat. We cannot leave here until tomorrow at the earliest.' His man hurried off to do his bidding.

'Why do you still look concerned, Kit? Surely she is safe away from here.'

'You are probably correct, my friend, but I think I shall be happier when I have made a few enquiries. Think about it, if they were indeed watching this place they would have seen her leave and followed her. I must be sure no strangers were seen either here or at the coaching inn before I can rest.'

He questioned any guests he could find but none of them had seen anything untoward. No pot-boy, stable boy or groom reported seeing strangers in the vicinity and certainly none had been asked any questions about Helena by strangers.

Duncan returned to tell them everything was ready inside. 'I shall borrow a horse and . . . '

'Allow me to do it for you, your grace, that is why you employ me.'

He was about to refuse but decided his man was as capable of carrying out this task as he was. 'Thank you, then I shall leave the matter in your capable hands.'

A substantial meal had been set out for them in the snug, which they devoured with relish. This place was relatively small so Theo and he would be obliged to share a chamber, but at least it was a decent size and the bed large enough to accommodate both of them.

'No baths, which does not surprise

me, but at least there is ample hot water. Hardly seems worth washing when we have nothing clean to put on afterwards,' Theo said gloomily.

'I look like a brigand and so do you. We might as well use the water whilst it's hot.'

He removed only his topcoat, cravat and boots and then fell onto the bed. He was instantly asleep. He was dragged from his slumber a short while later by Duncan hammering on the door and calling his name.

Instantly awake, he yelled for his man to enter. Theo was standing beside him, equally alert.

'Your grace, three men asked where her grace was going and then were seen to follow the coach.'

It was as if he had been punched in the chest. He was incapable of coherent thought, let alone speech. Then he gathered his wits. 'Duncan, do you have the route for this coach?'

'I do, your grace.'

'Where in God's name are we going

to find suitable horses?' His head was fuzzy, he wasn't sure how long he had been asleep but he was certain he would get no more rest for the foreseeable future.

'I have not been able to acquire any, but I have a post-chaise waiting outside. We will travel more quickly and can rest in between stops.'

Theo stepped forward and clapped Duncan on the back. 'You are a wonder, a marvel. Whatever you are being paid, it is not enough.'

They tumbled into the waiting vehicle and the driver snapped his whip and set off at a canter. Under normal circumstances, none of them would have been able to sleep when travelling at such speed. But they were all so fatigued that even the cramped space did not prevent them from sleeping.

There was nothing Kit could do until they reached the first stop which would be two hours from now. A week ago he had been the happiest of men, and now he was living in a nightmare. He had never aspired to be anything but Lord Drake, and because of something his long-deceased father had done, Helena was in danger. He would give up his title in a heartbeat to this murderous madman if that were possible.

The chaise rattled to a halt in the yard of the first inn. This would have been the first halt for the coach, where the horses would be changed but passengers would barely have had the time to alight and climb aboard before it departed again.

Duncan was out of the vehicle before either Kit or Theo was able to move. 'You are quite right to say my man is underpaid. He has always been more my man of affairs than my valet — in future he will only be the former and I shall appoint someone else to take care of my personal needs.'

'The horses are changed, we can be on our way as soon as he returns,' Theo replied.

Kit jumped down onto the cobbles to stretch his legs but he did not move far from the vehicle. There was no sign of his man. No doubt he was making enquiries both inside and out.

'Unless those men were intending to hold up the coach, I cannot see that Helena and her maid would be in any danger as long as they remained with the other passengers.'

'I think you are right, Kit, the danger will be when she has to transfer across town. She will be more vulnerable then.'

'In which case, why are we wasting time here? This is a lighter vehicle and travelling faster, she only left the inn three hours before our arrival so it is possible we could overtake them.'

Duncan raced towards them. 'No one saw any sign of those men.'

'As I thought.' Kit spoke to the man holding the ribbons. 'Do not do more than change the horses at each stop. I want to overtake the coach if possible.'

The coachman did not need telling he would be well-rewarded if he achieved this without killing all of them. Despite the discomfort of being bounced and tossed from side to side, all three of them managed to recuperate. He barely stirred when they stopped twice more for a fresh team.

They failed to catch up with their quarry on the road but he was hopeful they would arrive within a few minutes of the coach at the final destination. The noise and smell of the city was enough to bring them all to their senses.

He glanced around at his companions and was forced to smile. 'If I look as unkempt as you two, then I am a disgrace. I must be the only duke in the kingdom to look little better than a footpad.'

'Two days' growth of beard is not ideal, neither is the deplorable state of your garments,' Theo replied with a smile as he rubbed his own hand ruefully over his chin.

Duncan was hanging out of the window, looking ahead. 'We are almost there. I can see the roof of the coach over the wall. It cannot have arrived more than a few moments ago.'

'God willing, Helena will wish to go inside for refreshments before she hires a carriage to convey her to the coaching inn where she can catch her connection.'

The door was swinging open before the team had halted. Kit jumped out and raced for the inn, leaving Theo and Duncan to investigate the coach and speak to any remaining passengers. It was pandemonium in the spacious vestibule, but being taller than most gentlemen, Kit could see over the press of heads quite easily. Neither Helena nor her maid were in here.

How could this be? These passengers had only just alighted from the same coach she had been travelling on so she could not possibly have circumvented the queue and already have found herself a chamber. Nor could she have arranged for transport to her next destination in so short a time.

There was a constriction around his chest, his hands were clammy, and he had a very bad feeling about this.

*　*　*

Helena was heartily sick of the coach by the time they arrived in London. She had slipped the under-coachman a threepenny bit at the last halt and he knew to remove her trunk and the valise as soon as they arrived.

He did not let her down and their belongings were waiting for them to one side of the vehicle. There was an overwhelming smell of horseflesh, smoke and something far more unpleasant. London was not the place to be in the summer.

'You there, is your carriage for hire?' The driver nodded. 'Then kindly stow my luggage in your vehicle. I wish you to convey me to the Saracen's Head in Whitechapel.'

'Yes, miss, that will be one shilling and sixpence.'

Mary picked up the bag and the

driver hefted the small trunk into the well of the carriage. There was no need for steps and they scrambled in unaided. She was delighted that within a few minutes of her arrival she was already on her way to Whitechapel.

'I think it will be too late to travel tonight. I sincerely hope we can find accommodation at the inn.'

'I'll be glad to be on firm ground for a few hours before we're obliged to travel from Whitechapel to Chelmsford, my lady.'

'As shall I, I swear I shall not go anywhere in future unless I absolutely have to. My desire to gallivant around the countryside has quite evaporated.'

The hired carriage arrived at the Saracen's Head at the same time as the mail coach for Norwich. On enquiry she discovered there were two seats available if they wanted them. The trunk and bag were stowed with the other luggage at the rear of the vehicle and she had just sufficient time to visit the facilities before being obliged to step in and get settled for another uncomfortable journey.

The only other occupants were a married couple. The wife looked miserable and said nothing, the husband little better. Fortunately, they were respectably dressed and Helena was not unduly worried about travelling with them.

Then the coach door was opened and a rough-looking individual scrambled in. The couple refused to make room for him so he stepped over her feet and Mary's and squeezed himself into the corner beside her maid, who was in the central position. This man — he was certainly no gentleman — smelt unpleasant. The interior of the vehicle was already warm, and it would not be long before the atmosphere became most unpleasant.

The under-coachman was about to slam the door and remove the steps when she grabbed her maid's hand and jumped out. The steps were removed and the vehicle trundled out. 'That man was one of the villains trying to kill Lord Drake, I am almost certain of it. Quickly, we must find somewhere to hide. The others will be following the coach, waiting for their chance to murder me.'

Mary looked at her as if she were fit for bedlam. 'Your luggage, my lady, we have lost it.'

'Never mind about that, did you not hear what I just said? That man will jump out and look for us at the earliest opportunity.'

Her reticule was securely around her wrist so she had the wherewithal to find lodgings for the night. It could not be here, it would have to be somewhere less salubrious: this was the first place they would look when they returned.

'My lady, we should have stayed in the coach. Even if he was one of those chasing after you, how could he do you harm?'

'The other members of his gang were no doubt planning to masquerade as

248

highwaymen and hold the coach up when it went through Epping Forest.'

Mary wrung her hands. 'I thought it was Lord Drake they were trying to kill, why should they turn their attention to you?' She spoke without thinking of her position and on seeing Helena's expression immediately curtsied. 'I beg your pardon for speaking out of turn.'

'You are right to say that they did try and shoot his lordship. I am beginning to feel rather foolish. There could be no possible reason for them to follow me. We should have remained where we were. Too late to repine, we must now make the best of it.'

In her agitation, she had taken them both to the far side of the courtyard and they were standing in the shadows. As she was about to step forward, the man who had been sitting next to them ran into the yard. Her worst fears were realised. They were not wild imaginings at all.

*   *   *

She pressed herself against the wall and Mary did the same. They would be discovered if they remained where they were, so they must somehow find a way out of the yard without being seen. The ruffian rushed straight into the inn which gave them precious moments to make their escape.

'We cannot leave by the main entrance, we must find a way to get out at the back.'

Hand in hand they ran into the livery yard, past the coach house and found themselves in an enclosed area surrounded by high walls. Her heart was pounding. There could only be one explanation as to why the men had turned their attention to her — they intended to use her as a bargaining tool. Kit would sacrifice his own life without hesitation if it meant she was set free.

This was not going to happen. 'There must be a gate, a door, an exit, somewhere in this yard. The night soil men never enter through the front.' She shuddered at the thought of what that narrow alley would be like when they found it.

'Over here, my lady, it isn't locked.'

The stench was so bad Helena gagged and put her gloved hand over her mouth. Her eyes were watering, her stomach churning, but they had no choice.

She led the way, one hand over her mouth and the other holding up her skirts, doing the best she could not to step in anything the cart had dropped behind it. They emerged into a narrow lane which was slightly less noxious than the alleyway.

'There is a path leading between those buildings on the other side of the way. With luck it will take us onto a less frequented thoroughfare where we can find a smaller establishment to wait in.'

'I hope never to have to do anything so horrible again, my lady. There's a patch of grass over there where we can remove the worst from our boots. I have a cloth in my reticule.'

With the help of the cloth and the grass, Helena was sanguine that neither of them smelled of the midden. 'Thank the good Lord we were able to keep our hems from touching anything noxious. I doubt that even a smaller inn would be prepared to accommodate us otherwise.'

Eventually, they found sanctuary in a lodging house run by a widowed lady who assumed she was running away from an unwanted marriage. Helena did not disabuse her.

'There, madam, two jugs of hot water as you asked. I shall get my Sally to bring your supper on a tray. No one will find you here, you are safe in my house.'

'Thank you, Mrs Robinson. I reach my majority in three days' time and it will then be safe to leave here as I cannot then be coerced into something I do not wish to do.'

'I thought as much, my dear. Marriage to a gentleman one does not care for is not something I would recommend.'

13

Kit went into the building to enquire whilst Duncan and Theo asked questions in the yard. After a fruitless quarter of an hour, Theo was successful.

'I have just discovered Helena hired a carriage to take her to the Saracen's Head at Whitechapel. They left half an hour ago. God knows how much this jaunt has cost you, Kit; it is fortunate indeed that you are now as rich as Croesus.'

There was a fresh team harnessed and a third coachman. Kit wished he could get some proper shut-eye, but he would not rest until he had his beloved girl back in his arms. Their route through the city was speedy and he was able to discover that Helena had bought tickets on the Norwich coach which had left an hour ago.

If the men chasing him intended to abduct his wife in order to bring him into their line of fire, then they would do so in Epping Forest. He was almost too weary to contemplate further exertion. They needed food and a hot drink before they set off again. This time they would hire horses: they could travel more quickly that way.

Whilst Duncan went in search of mounts for them, he and Theo spoke to the landlord. 'I shall have a meal served to you in the private parlour, your grace. If I can be of further assistance in any way, do not hesitate to ask.' The man backed away, bowing as if in the presence of royalty. If he wasn't so damn tired he would have laughed.

The food was hot and more than adequate. The large jug of coffee was exactly what they wanted and adding generous measures of brandy to the dark, aromatic liquid enhanced its flavour. The parlour they were eating in overlooked the courtyard.

His eyes widened. He moved so

suddenly Theo dropped his coffee cup in his lap. 'Out there, I just saw three men ride in. I am certain they are the bastards we are looking for.' His relief that they had not found Helena was short-lived. If she had been on the coach, why were they back here searching the yard so frantically?

'Duncan, you are less conspicuous, I doubt they will recognise you. Drift out there and try and discover why they are here. There is something untoward taking place.'

One of the men was heading for the inn. 'God's teeth! I introduced you as the Duke of Andover. The landlord is bound to tell him you are here when he asks.'

Kit put his hand on Theo's arm. 'We are armed, rested and determined. This could be our chance. I shall resume my seat but have my loaded pistol ready under the table. You stand behind the door with yours primed and set.'

Duncan vanished through the small door the servants used. No doubt he was going in search of the third member of the group. There should be four of them — where the hell was the other one? He pushed the thought away and braced himself for action. He wasn't a violent man but was certain he could handle himself in a bout of fisticuffs. Whether he could actually shoot someone remained to be seen.

It was hard to pretend to be eating his meal, but this was essential if they were to surprise his would-be murderers. The door swung open. Before the two ruffians could do more than step inside, Theo had reversed his pistol and hit them both hard on the head. They collapsed like marionettes with broken strings.

Kit was on his feet and ripped off his neckcloth. He rolled the nearest figure on his front. Then he tied his ankles together and bent his legs and then attached his hands to his feet. Theo did the same with the other man.

'We need to stuff something in their mouths. The last thing we want is for them to start shouting and draw attention to the situation,' he said quietly.

'I am going to aid Duncan,' Theo replied. 'Here, stuff this handkerchief in one of their mouths.'

Kit did as suggested and then repeated the process with his own cotton square. His pulse had now returned to normal and he was able to view the situation more calmly. They needed to question one of the men, get absolute proof that their paymaster was the erstwhile Duke of Andover.

There was a scuffle outside the door and then a few thumps. The door crashed back and Theo and Duncan dragged in the missing man. They dumped him on the floor and proceeded to tie his hands and feet together, but this time in front of him.

'You have had the same thought as I. We need to be able to talk to one of them,' he said.

Duncan had closed the door and was leaning against it so no one could inadvertently interrupt them. He had scarcely put himself in position when there was a polite tap.

'I beg your pardon, your grace, is there something you need?' The landlord was outside.

'Everything is as it should be. I have no wish to be interrupted — is that quite clear?'

There was the shuffle of feet and then a response. 'Yes, your grace, you will be left to complete your business.'

'Excellent. You shall be well-rewarded for the use of your parlour.'

He waited until he was certain the landlord had retreated before turning to the job in hand. 'The one you fetched is coming round.' Kit snatched up one of the chairs, straddled it, and then folded his arms across the back and rested his head on them. In this position he looked almost benign. He intended to try a soft approach, to offer remuneration in return for information.

Theo took up a position on his right shoulder and Duncan on his left. They must make a formidable trio. The prisoner's eyes flickered open. He stared vacantly into space for a few seconds and then focused.

'Who sent you to kill me?'

The man shifted on his chair but made no reply. He was fully awake and looked to the side and saw the other members of his gang incapacitated.

Kit tried again. 'You have two options. Either you tell me willingly and I shall reward you or we will beat the information from you. Whatever happens, you will be incarcerated if you're lucky or dance at the end of a rope if you're not.'

One of the men tied up on the floor began to struggle. Duncan leaned down and hit him a second time without a qualm. The movement stopped.

'What sort of reward?'

'You will get half a crown for every answer that pleases me.'

The man dropped his chin on his chest and closed his eyes. These were battle-hardened ex-soldiers. They had been employed to murder him and possibly Helena as well. He must show no mercy. They would have shown none to him if they had had the opportunity to carry out their task.

He glanced over his shoulder and nodded to Duncan. His man stepped forward and kicked the chair over. The occupant landed painfully on his back and cursed them. The chair was righted and Kit tried again.

'I am the Duke of Andover. Your employer is at this very moment being arrested. Money in your pocket might make your life a little easier.' His tone was light but his expression hard.

'You already know that the man what wants to be the Duke of Andover employed us. He's a bad lot, a vicious cove and no mistake. I weren't happy about killing a maid but them other three would murder their own ma for a guinea.'

'Where is the fourth member of your gang?'

'I ain't rightly sure, yer grace, but

he's after your lady. She won't survive if he finds her.'

Somehow Kit managed to remain seated. There was something else he needed to know. 'Why did you come here?'

'The little lass jumped off the stage as it were leaving. Billy were inside with her, we was waiting down the road a bit. She'll not be far away and neither will he. I shouldn't stop here chatting to me, your honour, if you want to see your wife alive.' The man's evil laughter made his hair stand on end.

★ ★ ★

Helena hovered by the window of the lodging house, worried that one of those men would somehow find their way to her door.

'Come away, my lady, you will see nothing now it's dark. Allow me to close the curtains and then I can light the candles.'

'I think we are safe enough here; I am

certain my husband will come after me when he discovers that I have left that inn. But how will he be able to find me here? He will imagine the worst has happened but there is nothing I can do about it until the morning.'

'I'm going downstairs to collect your supper, my lady, and then I shall fetch water for your nightly ablutions.'

'Which reminds me, Mary, I wonder what happened to our luggage. In fact, I wonder where the trunks are at this very moment? This whole adventure has been fraught with disaster and I own I shall be glad when we are back at Faulkner Court.'

Supper was barely palatable, but she had little appetite anyway. She removed all her clothes and washed from top to toe. She disliked intensely being obliged to put back on grubby undergarments and a soiled travelling gown. Mary had suggested that they sleep in their petticoats but she was still not sanguine that those men would not find her. If they did break in she wished to be fully clothed.

The bed was big enough for both of them to sleep comfortably without the necessity of putting a bolster down the middle. However, she could not settle and had no wish to use the chamber pot when she was fully clothed.

Mary was sound asleep. A nearby church clock had just struck twelve — the street outside was deserted — it should be perfectly safe to visit the outside privy at this time of night. There was sufficient moonlight filtering in through the windows for her to find her way without the necessity of lighting a candle.

The door that led into the yard was bolted but they slid back easily and without making a noise. She had no wish to rouse the household and be obliged to explain what she was about. Her lips curved. There would be no need for any explanation as there could be only one reason a person ventured into the yard in the dark.

Fortunately, the night-soil men had

been recently and her visit was not too unpleasant. She re-bolted the back door and picked up her skirts so she could ascend the stairs safely. She had just reached the top when she heard a noise coming from the front parlour. She froze. What was it?

On tiptoes she moved until her back was pressed against the wall. She remained immobile, holding her breath, praying she had been mistaken. Then there was the unmistakable sound of a door opening downstairs. The men had discovered her whereabouts and at any moment would begin searching the house. Her fingers found the latch to her door, she lifted it and slipped inside. The sound of the bolt moving in the hasp was loud in the silence.

She moved swiftly to the bed and shook her maid awake. 'Mary, they have found us. They will be coming up the stairs at any moment. Quickly, help me barricade the door. We must somehow drag the chest of drawers across and position it in front.'

There was little point in worrying about the noise. Together they managed to move the chest and then piled every other item of furniture, apart from the bed, on top of it. 'If we drag the mattress and place it behind the chest we can sit on it, my lady, that will help keep the door closed.'

They had just collapsed onto this when someone rattled the door. 'There ain't no point in hiding, missy, the longer you keeps us waiting the worse it will be for you.' This whispered threat sent shivers down her spine.

Mary squeaked in horror and Helena pushed her fist into her mouth to prevent her doing likewise. Her maid clutched her hand and she held it tightly, giving them both much-needed courage.

Helena leaned down so she could speak softly and wouldn't be heard outside the chamber. 'They cannot get in; they dare not make a noise for fear of waking the household. The windows are too small for them to enter even if they could somehow reach them. We are safe. I shall not answer. All we have to do is sit here and remain quiet and we will be safe until Lord Drake comes to rescue us tomorrow morning.'

The girl stopped shaking. Helena had said this to offer comfort but realised as she spoke that if these men had found her then so would he.

The door was rattled again then all went quiet. Had they given up so easily? Then she heard the unmistakable sound of a tool of some sort being applied to the door hinges. She scrambled to her knees and inspected the barricade. With their combined weight and that of the furniture, even with the door removed she doubted they could get in.

Surely one of the lodgers who slept in the adjacent chambers must be able to hear the scratching and bumping coming from outside her door?

Suddenly the air was rent by an ear-splitting scream. 'Murder! Help!

Help, we are being murdered in our beds!'

This cry was taken up by three other women and the cacophony they made was deafening. 'The window, Mary, open it and scream as loud as you can. Sound travels in the darkness and with luck someone will hear and raise the alarm.'

With so much noise from the women inside, it was impossible to know if the would-be attackers had abandoned their attempt to get in or were still out there. They would be mad to remain.

'My lady, the night-watchman is coming. There are lights going on in the houses opposite. We are saved.'

It was a considerable time later before order was restored. Removing the pile of furniture had proved more difficult than putting it there — for some reason each item appeared to have doubled in bulk and weight. Eventually the door was free to open. The landlady appeared in her bedrobe looking less than pleased.

'That varmint who broke in has ruined my carpet and this door. I took you in, miss, out of the kindness of my heart, thinking you were an innocent miss hiding from an unwelcome suitor. That was no suitor — there's something havey-cavey about this business and I want no part of it. Leave my premises right now.'

'But, madam, we cannot wander the streets on our own at this time of night. I will recompense you for any damages.' There was no alternative but to reveal her identity. 'I am Lady Helena Drake, my husband is Lord Drake. I am hiding from an assassin.'

'And I am the king of England. I'll not hear any more of your nonsense, miss, you have caused me enough upset already. I'll not charge you for what you've had, nor for the breakages, I just want you gone from here this instant.'

There was no point in pleading. The woman was adamant. 'Is there a rear entrance we could depart by? Those men might well be waiting outside in the street for us. They were not captured by the constables.'

'As long as you leave I care not by which route you go. There is a gate at the side of the house that opens onto an alley. Follow that and it will bring you onto the main thoroughfare. You will be safe enough from harm on that.'

Helena, with Mary close behind, stumbled across the dark yard and eventually discovered the gate she had been told to leave by. 'This runs in both directions, I know not which way is the right one.'

'Listen, my lady, I think I can hear the sound of a carriage coming from the left.'

She listened and agreed this would be the best way to go. Fortunately, the dirt was dry and the path narrow enough for her to keep one hand on the wall to guide her and use the other to hold up her skirts. She emerged, blinking in the sudden change from complete darkness to the glow of lanterns hanging outside the entrances to the many inns.

She hesitated, not sure in which one she should seek sanctuary. 'I doubt we would be welcome wherever we go, but we cannot remain out here where we are easily seen.'

★ ★ ★

Kit, with Theo at his heels, erupted into the road. 'Where shall we start? Which way would she have gone?'

Before his friend could answer, the sound of shouting, pounding feet, and a general hue and cry echoed through the night. It came from a side street somewhere behind the one they were in. There was no need to ask his companion to follow, he was racing along beside him.

By the time they arrived, the disturbance was over but there were still lights on in one of the lodging houses. He hammered on the door and a disgruntled woman in her nightwear opened it.

'I'm looking for my wife, Lady Drake, is she here? Her life is in danger.'

'I sent her packing, I can't be doing with all that nonsense. Take the alley that runs between this house and the next one and you should find her.' The door was closed in his face without him being able to ask for an explanation.

He wished he'd had the foresight to bring a lantern as they were obliged to run full pelt in pitch darkness down the narrow track. He arrived first at the end of the alley. He looked in both directions and to his delight he saw his wife and her maid about to vanish around the corner.

'Helena, wait. I am here to take care of you.' His shout carried wonderfully and she reappeared. She picked up her skirts and raced towards him. He closed the gap equally fast and snatched her up.

'Darling girl, I cannot tell you how happy I am to see you safe. We have apprehended three of the men. Did the

271

fourth manage to find you?'

'He did, but he ran away when the night-watchman came. I should have stayed where I was . . . '

'Whether you were there or elsewhere you were equally at risk. I should have remained with you and not abandoned you as I did.'

Theo stepped up and made himself known. 'Sister, you have led us a merry dance, and I am relieved to find you safe and well after all the excitement.'

Kit put his arm firmly around her waist and led her back towards the Queen's Head, the inn where they had left the captured villains under the supervision of Duncan. Word had been sent to Bow Street and half a dozen constables had turned up to arrest the villains and take them away.

The landlord had yet to go to his bed. No doubt serving the wishes of a duke was worth remaining on duty for.

'Your man has bespoken three chambers, your grace. There is hot water awaiting you and a tray of refreshments will be sent immediately.'

Helena was staring at him. 'Your grace? Are you now a duke? Is this why someone wanted you dead?'

'It is, sweetheart. I hope you do not object to being a duchess.'

She smiled. 'There is little I can do about it, so why should I complain? I married you, not your title, whatever it might be.'

He told her all he knew as they ascended the stairs and she was remarkably relaxed about the whole thing.

The rooms allocated to his party were more than adequate. He was too fatigued to do more than gobble down the food, drink the coffee and then fall, fully clothed, onto the bed.

14

Helena did not have the heart to protest about Kit sleeping in his clothes but she drew the line at him still wearing his boots. These would have to come off and she had no intention of asking his valet to do it. What could be so difficult about taking off a gentleman's footwear?

She removed her bonnet, the brim that was once so crisp now sadly drooping, and tossed it onto a chair. Her gown was in little better shape, but it was the only one she had at the moment so that too must come off before she tackled the boots.

So, in her petticoats and bare feet she approached the bed. All thought of waking him fled when she saw the state of him. Not only was he covered in mud, but she had never seen him look so exhausted. He had been galloping about the countryside for hours so just this once she would allow him to sleep next to her as he was.

The room was warm, there was no need for her to find him a coverlet. He was sprawled on his back, his arms outflung, leaving her but a narrow space on the far side to sleep on. She carefully edged onto the bed but recoiled when she put her head on the pillow adjacent to his.

He smelt most unpleasant. She loved every inch of him, but not enough to lie beside him when he stunk so badly. Hastily she pulled away a pillow — she would have liked to have had the comforter, but no doubt it smelt as bad as he did now.

There was a perfectly adequate alternative for her to rest on. The daybed was where she would sleep for the remainder of the night. As she was drifting off to sleep he spoke in the darkness.

'My love, I have no wish to sleep alone . . . '

'In which case you had better remove your filthy garments and wash. I understand if you're too tired to do so, but do not expect me to sleep next to you.'

He muttered something extremely impolite and then there was the sound of him rolling out of bed. He cursed some more when he walked into an armchair, but then found the tinderbox and lit several candles.

'I shall do as you ask, sweetheart.' He shrugged out of his jacket and dropped it on the floor. His shirt and waistcoat followed. She was sitting up watching this display with interest. He held out his arm and sniffed it.

'Devil take it! I smell like a midden.'

He then sat on the bed and attempted to remove his boots. They refused to budge.

'I shall do it for you, Kit, but I can assure you it is with great reluctance that I approach so close to you.'

She turned her back and once his leg was between hers she grasped his boot.

To her annoyance he put his other foot on her bottom and as she pulled, he shoved. The result was that when his boot flew across the room, so did she. She glared at him over her shoulder as she pushed herself up from the floor.

'If you expect me to repeat that performance, your grace, you are sadly mistaken.'

His chuckles did nothing to help the situation. 'I apologise most wholeheartedly, my dear, but I cannot think of another way to remove my footwear.'

'In which case, your grace, the second boot must remain on your foot.'

'Then I shall have no option but to call Duncan to do it. I think you might wish to put on your gown before he arrives.'

An impasse. Then she saw what he must surely have already noticed: there was a boot iron attached to the fender that he could have used for the first one.

'It is very warm in here, I think I might remove my petticoats as well. I do hope your valet will not object to seeing me unclothed?' She smiled sweetly at him.

'*Touché*, my love. I should know better than to tease you as I think you are beginning to outwit me on that score.'

He removed his second boot with no problems, using the iron to hook it off. Then her eyes widened as he stripped off his breeches and strolled with nothing on at all to the washstand. 'I suppose I cannot ask you to assist me with my ablutions?'

'You certainly cannot.' She crossed over to the bed and sniffed loudly. 'The linen is already quite ruined by your resting on it in your dirt. I shall sleep on the *chaise longue* as planned.'

There was a second comforter folded neatly on the end of the bed and she took this with her. She plumped the pillow, wrapped herself in the cover, and then with a sigh of satisfaction settled down to sleep. She had scarcely closed her eyes when she was rudely awakened.

'This will not do, this will not do at all. Up you come, my love, you have the inestimable honour of spending the night in the same bed as the Duke of Andover. I can imagine how honoured you must feel at this privilege.'

The room was dark again as he had snuffed the candles, but she was well aware he was laughing down at her. She was also well aware he was still stark naked. 'To be honest, I find that I am not overfond of the duke, I much preferred Lord Drake.'

She was dumped unceremoniously into the centre of the bed and he joined her there. 'My darling, I find that I am quite restored after my wash. Now, I believe you said that you were hot and wished to remove your petticoats.'

A considerable time later she fell asleep, where she belonged, in his arms.

*　*　*

Kit woke after a few hours and gently removed Helena's arms from his person and then slid out of bed. There were things he needed to do before she woke. He was hopeful the luggage that had travelled without her on the coach would have been returned by now. His three men, and his own carriage, should also be making its way in their general direction. It would, of course, arrive on the wrong side of town, which was one reason he had risen so early.

Theo was down before him and tucking into a hearty breakfast in the snug. There was no sign of Duncan. 'Good morning, my friend, I take it you have sent Duncan to collect the carriage.'

'He left half an hour ago, he should be back with your luggage in time for you to change your raiment. You can hardly appear in public as you are. Seeing a duke in such disarray will cause consternation throughout the *ton*.'

'You are in little better case, Theo, so let us hope your men also arrive. Presumably they have what you need in their saddlebags.'

'Then we have only to find the missing man and this matter will be settled. My cousin will now be Lord Drake I suppose. I presume that my sisters and mother have also been elevated — they have become ladies and Mama is now the Dowager Duchess of Andover.'

'They are indeed. Do you intend to write to your mother and explain the circumstances or wait until you return and can do it in person?'

'I need to speak to my lawyers. I want to be fully informed before I take up my new position. There is one thing that I cannot understand. Why did my uncle reveal his secret on his deathbed? If he had remained silent then things would have continued as they have these past twenty-five years.'

'Your legal team will no doubt be able to answer all your questions. Your breakfast has arrived. They must have seen you come down. It is astonishing how much better the service is for someone as toplofty as yourself.'

The landlord informed him that a man had come with the missing box and bag, and these had been taken up for Helena and her maid. There had been no word from Duncan that his trunk was on its way. He could hardly wander about the place so dishevelled.

Instead he had sent a message for his lawyers to attend him where he was. He cared not if they were shocked by his malodorous appearance — they were there to do his bidding and not pass judgement on himself. They would not be here for another hour at least — time enough for him to see Helena.

He had never been happier. Since he took over the family estate it had been a constant battle to keep the creditors at bay. For the first time in his adult life he would have sufficient funds to take care of his people and give his wife and family the life of luxury they deserved.

He knocked on the door of their shared chamber but received no response. Puzzled, but not unduly worried, he opened the door. The room was empty. There was no dressing room, no sitting room, and he was certain she had not come downstairs. Was this a game she was playing? He was about to call her name when he saw something that filled him with dismay.

In the centre of the room was a valise and small trunk, but they were not the ones belonging to Helena. For a few seconds his brain refused to function. He could not take in the evidence he was staring at. The remaining rifleman had abducted Helena. There could be no other explanation for what he saw in front of him.

Then he heard a noise coming from under the bed. He dropped to his knees and gently extricated the maid. There was a hideous bruise on her temple and she was semi-comatose. He placed her on the bed and then charged from the room, taking the stairs two at a time.

He saw the landlord. 'My wife has been kidnapped, her maid has been injured. Take care of her.'

Theo was finishing his coffee and reading yesterday's newspaper. He took one look at Kit's face and was on his feet. 'Tell me — what has happened?'

Kit explained. 'God knows how he got in, or how he got her out without being seen.'

'It makes no sense. What can he hope to gain by doing this? His paymaster has already been taken into custody as far as we know.'

'Ransom? He must be acting of his own volition.' His heart began to slow as he considered the situation without panic. 'He will not harm her, Helena is more valuable to him alive than dead.'

'You are correct. All we have to do is wait for the note or the message and then . . . '

'Wait? Have you taken leave of your senses? I intend to find her and the bastard will not survive the encounter.'

The first thing he had to do was discover how the abduction had taken place right under his nose. 'Theo, make enquiries in the yard. Someone must have seen this man turn up with the box and bag. I shall be inside.'

He hurtled back to the empty room, intending to make a systematic search. He had forgotten the injured girl who was now being attended to. A smartly dressed, grey-haired woman looked up as he burst in. 'Your grace, the physician has been sent for. I do not believe your servant will die from this injury.'

'Excellent. I wish to know how my wife was removed from here without anyone being aware of it.'

The woman moved to his side, her complexion pale, her expression worried. 'We have a secondary staircase, it is at the rear of the building and leads directly to the stables. It is used for bringing in the luggage.'

She wrung her hands. 'The man came to the back door and said he had been sent to deliver the missing boxes for her grace. It was I who told him which chamber to take them to.'

'I do not apportion blame to you, madam. How long ago did he come up here?'

'No more than half an hour ago, your grace. I have already sent out all my available staff to make enquiries on your behalf.'

Kit emerged from the backstairs into a flagstone passageway. It was directly opposite the door that led into the stables. He ran out into the street, but it was deserted. Not even a passing diligence or pedestrian from whom he could obtain information. There must have been a carriage waiting otherwise someone would have seen the man carrying Helena. She would have struggled, made a racket if she could have — therefore, he must conclude that she too had been knocked unconscious.

There was a clatter of feet behind him and Theo burst out. 'Is this the way he took her?'

'I believe so. There's little point in us racing about like madmen when we have no inkling which way to go.' He thought for a moment before continuing. 'The landlord's wife has already sent out several men and boys to make enquiries up and down the street. We have to wait and pray they have found her.'

Theo put his arm around Kit's shoulders. 'Then will you return to the snug to wait for news? Duncan has gone to Bow Street and there will be a general hue and cry throughout the city. They will find Helena and she will be returned to you before the day's end, I am sure of it.'

With leaden feet he returned to the inn and followed the passageway around to the front of the building. As he arrived in the commodious vestibule, two black-garbed gentlemen carrying documents walked in. They were his lawyers. He was about to ask his friend to send them away but reconsidered. Having something to think about other than his missing love would be a good thing.

He nodded and they bowed. He didn't need to ask them to follow him. 'Do you wish me to remain with you or shall I . . . '

'I doubt I shall take anything in. I should be grateful if you would sit in with me and hear what they have to say.'

Mr Frobisher and the unidentified clerk were horrified to be told that Helena had been kidnapped. Kit had no time for their sympathy — in fact, he had no wish to listen to anything they had to say. He settled himself by the window so he could watch the yard and left his brother-in-law to speak to them.

Their conversation washed over him until they answered a question Theo had put; it was one he had been asking himself. 'It is all very confusing, my lord. It would appear that the gentleman who has been masquerading as the Duke of Andover for the past twenty-six years did not wish his son to inherit the title and estates as the man is a profligate, a gambler, a rake — the worst kind of person you could imagine. Quite unsuitable to hold the rank of duke.

'For this reason he told the truth on his deathbed to his lawyers and to his son. I am certain he would not have done so if he had known what the outcome of such an announcement would be.'

Kit straightened and went to join them. 'Are you saying he would not have renounced his title?'

'No, your grace, I am certain that he would have. I meant that he would not have told his son until matters had been arranged.'

'If the man knew his son to be inherently bad, he must have known how he would react. I think he wanted this to happen — to have the family ripped apart . . . '

'Kit, you are talking nonsense. Your grief and worry are addling your wits.'

The door flew open and Duncan appeared. 'He has been found. Two of the stable boys were able to locate the carriage he used. He is holding her gracc in an empty building no more than a mile from here. One of them is watching outside, the other returned here to tell us.'

Kit barged past his man and was in the yard before he had finished speaking. The stable boy, red-faced from his running, was standing outside. A stout gentleman had just dismounted from his cob and was about to hand the reins to the lad.

'I must borrow this horse, sir, and this boy.' He vaulted into the saddle and reached down and swung the boy up behind him. 'Which way?'

The welcome weight of his loaded pistol banged against his thigh. He would have need of it shortly.

*   *   *

Helena opened her eyes but could see nothing, nor could she breathe freely. Her heart was pounding, her head ached abominably and she couldn't think for a moment what was happening. Then she recalled that dreadful moment when the man who had fetched in the trunks had turned on Mary and knocked her out. Then before she had gathered her wits he had done the same to her. After that she had no notion what had transpired.

She remained still, she did not wish him to know she had come around. There was a noxious bag over her head and her limbs were restrained by ropes. From the bouncing and noise, they were travelling at speed in a carriage of some sort.

If only her head was clear she might be able to think what best to do. Then her befuddled brain began to function a little better. There had only been one man, so he could not be in two places at once. If he was driving then she was alone inside. She was jammed into the well of the carriage, with her back against the door.

Surely she should be able to sense his presence, touch his feet with hers, if he was indeed inside with her? Did she dare risk trying to wriggle out of her bonds? She was about to move when she was kicked viciously in the side.

'I knows you're awake, missy, so don't you try nothing or it'll be the worse for you.'

Immediately she was still. This meant there were at least two men involved in her capture. Had the four of them orchestrated this event together? There was no point in her trying to escape. She would have to pray that Kit and Theo came to her rescue before she was harmed.

The vehicle did not travel for long; they could not be more than a mile from the inn where she had been staying. She was tempted to feign unconsciousness but thought it might get her rougher treatment if she made him carry her.

Even with a bag over her head she was obliged to hold her breath when he leaned down to untie the ropes that held her. 'Up you come, missy, we've a nice place to hide you away until we gets our dues.'

He dragged her from the carriage and she cracked her knee, her shins and her elbows as she was pulled through the door. Then he pushed her along in front of him. This was terrifying as she could not see where she was going.

Up steps, down steps, through a large, empty, dank-smelling space, and then she was forced to ascend a flight of stairs. She was shoved in the back and fell on her knees. A door slammed behind her. Frantically she worked at the twine that was around her neck, holding the bag in place. Eventually she managed to undo the knot and snatched it from her head.

The room was about three yards square and had a small window too high for her to reach. There was a faint glimmer of light through it which made the space less oppressive. There was no furniture, nothing to sit on and if she needed to answer a call of nature, she would have to do it in the corner as there was no receptacle provided.

She slid down the wall, oblivious to the state of the floor. That was the least of her worries. The man had said he was expecting to be paid to release her — she hoped this was the truth. She could identify him. This might make him think he had better . . . she could not complete the thought.

No, there was nothing to worry about on that score as her beloved husband and her brother would arrive at any moment. She prayed they would bring sufficient men to release her. Would the men who had been left behind arrive in time to accompany them?

There was nothing she could do except wait and be ready to leave without a fit of the vapours when she was released.

15

The boy clung on grimly to Kit's waist and was able to yell his instructions as they galloped through the streets. He pulled his sturdy mount to a rearing halt at the end of the road that led to the building Helena was held in.

'It's the one on the right, your grace, at the far end of the track.'

'You're quite certain of that? If you are correct then where is the other boy?'

'He went inside, your grace, there's a doorway. He'll find you right enough once you're inside.'

'Right. Can you ride?'

'I can, your grace.'

'Good. Return to the inn and then lead the others here.' Kit dismounted and watched the lad scramble into the saddle. 'Put your feet in the loop of leather above the iron, that should be sufficient to keep you steady.'

'I ain't bothered about no stirrups, your grace, I can ride without them.'

Kit waited until the horse was thundering in the opposite direction before beginning his stealthy approach. He moved in the shadows, sure he wouldn't be seen at this distance by anyone keeping watch. He removed his pistol, primed and loaded it. Then, with it held securely by his right side, he continued.

This area was deserted, not even a mangy dog or cat. On both sides of the narrow dirt track there were looming buildings. They were mostly derelict with gaping holes in the roof and sagging walls. In the distance he could hear the shouts of the dock workers unloading cargo from a newly docked ship.

He arrived at an entrance; if it had had a door at one time, it certainly did not now. He pressed himself against the wall and listened for the slightest sound within. He did not doubt for one second that the boy had brought him to the correct place.

He could hear nothing suspicious so ventured through the doorway. Ahead of him was a narrow, dark passageway leading to God knows where. There was a glimmer of light at the far end, and still nothing to indicate if he was expected or in imminent danger. Where the hell was the other lad? If anything had happened to him he would never forgive himself.

Light filtered in from unglazed openings at intervals on the inside wall which made it less hazardous, but also meant that if the kidnapper appeared at the far end, he would be clearly visible and have nowhere to hide. He had no option but to creep along the passage. He was halfway down when a small face suddenly appeared above him, causing him to drop his pistol.

'You got here quick, your grace,' he whispered. 'I weren't expecting you so soon. You don't want to go to the end, there's one of the varmints watching it.

You need to climb through here like what I did.'

Kit viewed the opening and doubted his broad shoulders would fit through. 'How many am I dealing with, do you know?'

'Two, your grace. One's got a rifle and the other don't have no weapon apart from a cudgel.'

'Here, take my gun. It's loaded so be careful.' He handed it up and once he was sure that the boy had moved away, he grasped the edge of the window and heaved himself upwards. He did this with such force he lost his grip and tumbled through headfirst to land in an undignified heap at the urchin's feet.

'Well, you did that right smart, sir.' His weapon was returned to him and he dropped it back into his topcoat pocket.

'Is my wife unharmed?'

'That she is, sir. She's in a small storeroom what you have to go upstairs to get to. She ain't making no noise, not crying nor wailing and she was walking all right, but had a right nasty bag over her head.'

'Do you have any idea exactly where the two men are at this moment?'

'I do, your grace. The rifleman's on the roof and the other cove's sitting on the stairs. You'll have to get round him.'

A wave of white-hot fury flooded him. The man on the roof was waiting to kill him when he came with the money for the ransom. The fact that Helena was still unharmed was not through the goodness of their hearts but the fact that they were keeping her for themselves.

'I don't know your name.'

'Ned, sir, Ned Smith.'

'Then, Ned Smith, this is what you must do. Climb back through this window and wait out of sight at the end of the road. You must tell whoever comes to leave their horses where they cannot be seen and then approach in the shadows, keeping flat against the wall.'

The boy nodded and grinned. 'If

you'd be so kind as to give me a shove, I reckon I can do it.'

Kit picked him up and held him above his head so he could push Ned out feet first. He waited until the boy tapped on the wall to say he was down and then cocked his pistol and headed for the stairs.

He walked soft-footed in the direction he had been told. Sure enough, the second thug was lounging at the top of the staircase, his cudgel across his knees. It would be better to knock him out, but there was no way he could approach him without being seen.

He stepped around the corner, cocking his gun loudly. The sound was unmistakable and had the desired effect. Kit was a deadly shot. He could, from this distance, shoot the man through the heart if necessary.

'I am the Duke of Andover. You will release my wife without a fuss if you wish to live.'

The man was obviously slow-witted. Whilst he was still thinking, Kit bounded up the stairs, reversed his gun and knocked him senseless. Then he rummaged through his pockets and removed the key to the padlock that held the door shut.

'Helena, sweetheart, I have come to take you home.' Immediately he heard movement behind the door.

'I am unhurt, my love. A trifle pungent, but nothing worse I do assure you.'

He unlocked the door and she flew into his arms. He pulled her close, his heart hammering, his legs weak from relief and joy. 'We must not linger here, darling girl, but make our escape as soon as we can.'

He pushed her through the window but she was too heavy for him to do it the same way as he had for the lad. She vanished, feet kicking and petticoats flying, to land with a thud on the other side of the wall. They were making too much noise and taking too long. He followed her headfirst and this time was prepared and rolled, rather than sprawled.

'I must check my pistol, it won't take me a moment.' Once this was done he grabbed her hand and they ran to the exit. They were yards from safety when a bullet slammed into the wall no more than inches from his head.

He threw himself flat, taking her down with him so he was lying across her, using his body to protect her from harm. He had one chance. If he remained alive until the man was within range, he could shoot him. Another bullet smacked into the dirt, this time a foot from him.

'Roll with me; we must get closer to the wall. It will be harder for him to hit us there.' They did so and he was certain that without a lantern the shooter could only be guessing as to their whereabouts. The passageway was dark and up against the wall, with their faces turned away, he prayed they would be almost invisible.

It took only half a minute to reload a rifle. Why hadn't he shot again? Then a voice he recognised called from where the man had been.

'He's dead, your grace, you are both safe to stand.' Duncan had somehow managed to approach from the rear and surprise the assassin.

* * *

Helena was too shocked to do more than lean against Kit. Her head was spinning, she could hardly take in what had transpired over the past hour. Everything had happened so fast.

Her brother hugged them both. 'I thank God for your safety, my dear. I shall leave you to talk and we can reconvene shortly at the inn.'

'Is it over, Kit?'

'Sweetheart, the other three men are in jail — the fourth is dead. Their paymaster has been forced to flee the country. We are safe.'

'Could he not come back when no one is watching?'

'When I say he fled the country, that

is not strictly accurate. What actually happened was that he was given the option of hanging or going into exile and, not surprisingly, he chose the latter. He was allowed to take his horse and a bag of gold. If I had met him first he would not have survived the meeting.'

'How bloodthirsty you are, my love. I had not thought you a violent man. If he had not tried to kill both of us what would have happened?'

They had now reached their carriage and once they were safely inside, they resumed their conversation. 'As we are travelling in our own carriage, are we to assume that we now have our luggage and all your men?'

'We do indeed. We shall both bathe and be able to put on fresh garments for the first time in three days. We shall remain where we are tonight, but tomorrow we must go to Andover Hall. I have papers to sign in order to take up my new position. I was in the middle of a meeting with my lawyers when you were abducted. They are waiting for me to return so that everything can be set in motion.'

'I should have asked immediately: how is Mary? I remember her being struck down before I was knocked out myself.'

'The doctor had been called but the landlord's wife was confident your girl had not been seriously injured. Although she might not be well enough to accompany us to our new residence in Hertfordshire.'

'Then I shall wait with her until she is fully recovered. I can hardly travel without a personal maid now that I am the Duchess of Andover.' Her comment was meant to be taken lightly but he thought her serious.

'You are quite right, my love, I shall have to appoint . . . '

'No, Kit, you will not. I have told you that I intend to wait until Mary is recovered. If you are in such a rush to depart then you must do so without me. I will come when I am able to.'

The arm around her shoulders was withdrawn and he turned her around to face him, a difficult accomplishment in the confines of a carriage, using both hands. She held her breath, not sure if she was going to be taken to task for disagreeing with him or if he was going to apologise.

'How can you be so calm after what you have been through? I cannot imagine there is another young lady in the land with such courage as you. Of course, there is no reason to hurry. Until two days ago I was unaware of my lofty position in society.'

'I am calm, my darling, because I was in no danger. I was certain that you would come and find me before I could be harmed. I should like to add, whilst we are on the subject, that Duncan is a remarkable man. Perhaps it is you that needs a new valet as he should immediately be promoted to something that suits his abilities.'

His hands tightened slightly. He was annoyed at her impertinence. Then he relaxed. 'He is also my man of business — and you are quite correct, it is I that need a new manservant, not you that needs a new abigail.'

He kissed her, not passionately, but tenderly and was about to pull her onto his lap when the carriage turned sharply into the yard of the inn.

The door was opened with a flourish and the steps let down. 'Good heavens! There must be a dozen men milling about in here and I recognise most of them. Are we to travel with so many? It will look like a small army or the arrival of royalty.'

He handed her down and then followed. 'Theo's men will return to Faulkner Court but my three will accompany us when we leave. I am hoping that your brother will agree to come as well. As the heir to an earldom he is better placed than me to assess what might need doing in my new demesne.'

'Well, they cannot remain here, that is for sure. I shall write a letter to my parents explaining what has transpired — do you think they can wait until that is done before they depart?'

'They will leave when they are told to,' he said with a smile.

She raced upstairs and into the bedchamber. She was delighted to see Mary sitting up in bed, drinking tea. The girl was so shocked she dropped the cup. 'Your grace, I beg your pardon, I shouldn't be in your bed, I shall go immediately . . . '

Helena ran to her side, removed the cup and then took her hands. 'Enough, you must remain here until you are well. His grace and I will no doubt be transferring to his London home. You will join us there when you are fully recovered.'

There was no sign of her luggage and she would dearly like to change her clothes. There was a tap on the door and Kit opened the door but did not come in. He nodded to Mary who slithered back under the covers. Helena hurried to join him in the passageway as she could not talk freely in front of her girl.

'I have told Mary she will be taken care of here until she can join us wherever we are. I assume there is somewhere in town that your family owns?'

'There is indeed. We have a house in Grosvenor Square; our baggage has already been transferred there and the staff warned of our arrival. Are you ready to leave, sweetheart?'

The house in Grosvenor Square was a magnificent building, set back from the street and in a prestigious position, but one look was enough to tell her all was not well.

'Kit, the windows are filthy, the steps have not been scrubbed for weeks. If that is the calibre of the staff then I have no wish to reside here even for one night. Can we not stay at Grillon's?'

'Unfortunately not. Our trunks are already here. Hopefully, Theo has things in hand. I cannot see even the most recalcitrant of servants refusing to obey his instructions.'

The door opened as they arrived on the top step. However, it was not opened by a smart butler, but by Duncan himself. His expression was grim.

'The place has been abandoned, your grace. There are no staff to serve you. Lord Faulkner is trying to rectify that matter. Our men are doing their best to find you a chamber.'

They had scarcely moved inside when there was a thunderous knocking on the front door. Duncan returned to open it and an elegant couple burst in. The gentleman was tall, broad-shouldered and fair-haired. The lady, dark-haired and quite beautiful, was dressed in the first stare of fashion.

'Your grace, forgive me for arriving so precipitously. Allow me to introduce myself. I am Rochester, Earl of Medway and this is my wife. You cannot possibly stay here. Please would you do me the honour of coming next door to my house?'

Kit nodded to both. 'Having seen the

state of the place I cannot tell you how pleased I am to be invited to reside elsewhere. I had not thought to find any of the houses occupied at this time of year.'

Lady Rochester smiled at both of them. 'We would not normally be in town in the summer but there is a concert we wish to attend.'

Rochester turned and snapped his fingers and half a dozen liveried footmen stepped in. 'They will transport your belongings.'

'Forgive me, my lord, but I cannot abandon my brother, Lord Faulkner, who is with us.'

'Of course, he must come too.'

He glanced nervously at her husband but he nodded and smiled. She moved forward so she could converse with her hostess, leaving the gentlemen to do the same.

'I am surprised that you knew who we are, my lady.'

'Your man sent word to us of your arrival. I think he was hopeful we would extend an invitation as the house is in an appalling state, not fit for habitation. I cannot tell you how pleased we are that we no longer have that man living next door.'

Within a very short space of time, Helena was luxuriating in a lemon-scented bath and being attended to by an excellent abigail. By the time her hair was dry and dressed, an unconscionable time had passed. She was not surprised to see an evening gown had been put out for her.

'Your grace, I took the liberty of selecting this one. I hope I have chosen something that you like.'

'It is exactly right. I hope I am not tardy, I should hate to keep everyone waiting for dinner.'

'His grace is in your sitting room, your grace, he has only just arrived.'

★ ★ ★

Kit had been ready an hour before his beloved but was glad to be able to converse with Theo. 'There is something I wish to ask you first. I need to tell you that I have put Duncan in charge of the restoration of my town house. He will join me when things are as they should be here. My sisters will be coming out next year and the house must be ready by then.'

'I know what you're going to ask me. And the answer is an unequivocal yes.' His friend smiled. 'You want me to accompany you and Helena to Andover Hall. Wild horses could not keep me away. It is not every day that one's closest friend unexpectedly becomes a duke.'

'I have signed all the necessary papers, letters have been sent to everyone who needs to know. From what I have learned about my cousin I am glad he did not hold the title for long. My uncle was a decent enough duke and took care of his estates, houses and people.'

'Would you like me to return to collect your mother and sisters after I have seen you settled?'

'That was the other thing I intended to ask you. I gather that Andover Hall is a vast barracks of a place. I am seriously considering razing it to the ground — but not until I have had built something modern, something that Helena will be comfortable in.'

She had overheard his comment as she came in through her bedchamber door. 'What do you wish me to be comfortable in, my love?'

He stared at her, for a moment unable to think coherently or recall what he had been speaking of. He had always thought her an attractive young lady; he decided she was quite beautiful the day he understood he loved her. But tonight, in a stunning confection of silver sparkles over a pale blue skirt, her hair arranged in a sophisticated style, he was made speechless by her beauty.

Theo poked him sharply in the ribs. 'Answer her. You are staring at my sister like a lovesick boy.'

It was as if there were only the two of

them in the room. She glided towards him and he held out his hands. She ignored them and moved smoothly into his arms. 'I love you so much, Kit, but are you sure that you don't regret your decision? You are now a duke and I am concerned that I won't be able to be the sort of duchess that everyone will expect you to have.'

He tilted her head and kissed her. 'I am as anxious as you, sweetheart, about how to act appropriately. I love you; you will be the perfect duchess and if anyone says anything to the contrary they will have me to answer to.'

Books by Fenella J. Miller
in the Linford Romance Library:

THE RETURN OF LORD RIVENHALL
A COUNTRY MOUSE
A RELUCTANT BRIDE
A DANGEROUS DECEPTION
MISTAKEN IDENTITY
LORD ATHERTON'S WARD
LADY CHARLOTTE'S SECRET
CHRISTMAS AT HARTFORD HALL
MISS SHAW & THE DOCTOR
TO LOVE AGAIN
MISS BANNERMAN AND THE DUKE
MISS PETERSON & THE COLONEL
WED FOR A WAGER
AN UNEXPECTED ENCOUNTER
HOUSE OF DREAMS
THE DUKE'S PROPOSAL
THE DUKE'S RELUCTANT BRIDE
THE DUKE & THE VICAR'S
DAUGHTER
LORD ILCHESTER'S INHERITANCE
LADY EMMA'S REVENGE
CHRISTMAS AT CASTLE ELRICK
A MOST UNUSUAL CHRISTMAS

THE RECLUSIVE DUKE
A LORD IN DISGUISE
CHRISTMAS AT DEVIL'S GATE
A MOST DELIGHTFUL CHRISTMAS
CHRISTMAS GHOSTS AT
THE PRIORY
A CHRISTMAS BETROTHAL

We do hope that you have enjoyed reading this large print book.

Did you know that all of our titles are available for purchase?

We publish a wide range of high quality large print books including:
**Romances, Mysteries, Classics
General Fiction
Non Fiction and Westerns**

Special interest titles available in large print are:
**The Little Oxford Dictionary
Music Book, Song Book
Hymn Book, Service Book**

Also available from us courtesy of Oxford University Press:
**Young Readers' Dictionary
(large print edition)
Young Readers' Thesaurus
(large print edition)**

For further information or a free brochure, please contact us at:
**Ulverscroft Large Print Books Ltd.,
The Green, Bradgate Road, Anstey,
Leicester, LE7 7FU, England.
Tel:** (00 44) **0116 236 4325**
Fax: (00 44) **0116 234 0205**

A YEAR IN JAPAN

Patricia Keyson

When ex-librarian Emma announces she's accepted a year-long position to teach English in Japan, the news shocks her grown children. Enjoying single life after half a year of estrangement from her husband Neil, Emma can't wait to embark upon her adventure in three weeks. Then Neil is hospitalised after a car accident, and needs a carer at home while he recovers. Emma is the only one available to help. Three weeks — can Neil make up for lost time before Emma leaves, and will she let him back into her heart?

GRANDPA'S WISH

Sarah Swatridge

Melanie is growing tired of her job at a family law firm, until she is tasked with tracing a Mr Davies, the beneficiary of a late client's estate. Tracking him down, Melanie is surprised to find Robbie-Joe uninterested in the terms of the will, especially when he learns that it belonged to a grandfather he had no idea existed. To claim his fortune, Robbie-Joe must complete twelve challenges in twelve months. But Melanie has a challenge of her own: to stop her feelings for Robbie-Joe becoming anything more than professional . . .

HOME TO MISTY MOUNTAIN

Jilly Barry

UK-born Hayley Collins is visiting Australia, staying with a friend and looking for work. Craig Maxwell runs a holiday resort at Misty Mountain, a four-hour drive from Melbourne. When Hayley applies to be an administrator at the resort, Craig takes her on — and much else besides. She has to return to England in twelve months. He's engaged to a woman whose father is helping to keep the resort's finances in the black. So when Hayley and Craig fall in love, it seems a future together is only a distant dream . . .

RUBY LOVES . . .

Christina Garbutt

Crime writer Adam finds the peace he needs to finish his latest novel in a remote stately home in Carwyn Bay, Wales — at least until effervescent, disaster-prone Ruby arrives to run the tourist café while also pursuing a secret plan to uncover her grandfather's past. Through baking disasters and shocking revelations, they find themselves falling in love. But Ruby is saddened by what she learns about her grandfather, and plans to go home to America at the end of the summer. Will their relationship be strong enough to last?